SERVANT OF THE LUST DEMON

Daniel L. Darke

SERVANT OF THE LUST DEMON

GRAVESTONE PRESS

Chapter 1

Everyone who knew Sam Hughes always suspected that he would meet his death at the hands of a jealous husband.

Sam saw no reason to think otherwise. He had been obsessed with women for more than half of his thirty-two years and had learned long ago that nearly every female he was attracted to was going through life with a horde of issues. Some of these concerns came in the form of mental or behavioral problems while others dealt with more dangerous realities, such as husbands or boyfriends. Sam's downfall was that he simply did not care. If a woman flicked his *on* switch, he simply went after her.

Sam was not tall, handsome, or athletically built. Slender and slightly pale, he was of average height and looks. However, his baby face, thick dark-brown hair, light blue eyes, and harmlessly soft manner served him well. Women noticed him wherever he went. Most experienced the instinctive need to protect him. To hold him in their arms and chase his demons away. To them, he was the deceptive-looking bad boy they had always been warned about or the brother they had always wanted to consume but couldn't.

Sam welcomed their advances with the enthusiasm of a starving man accepting food scraps tossed in his lap. He had lived and dreamed sex ever since he was old enough to experience his first erection. He lost his virginity at age twelve, to the older sister of a neighborhood friend. The girl's name was Janice. She was a flirtatious eighteen and should have known better. Like Sam, she didn't seem to care about behavioral problems or principles. She considered him just as cute and as cuddly as the fluffy, one-eyed teddy bear she had slept with as a child and had no qualms about pulling him into the back seat of her ancient Ford Fairlane just fifteen minutes after meeting and talking to him.

Ever since that day, Sam had successfully nailed every woman he had ever wanted.

Ursula interested him from the first moment he laid eyes on her. Tall, slender, and almond-eyed, Ursula worked as the attending R.N. of St. Cloud Hospital, where Sam went for X-rays one Saturday morning after hurting his shoulder lifting boxes in the mailroom at work.

Hot-blooded, with strong urges and a natural compulsion to flirt, Ursula took to Sam immediately. According to her, Sam favored her very first boyfriend Donald, who had died fifteen years earlier, in Iraq. And since her husband, a successful pawnshop owner in Kissimmee, had flown to Miami on a business trip, leaving her alone for several days, Ursula saw no reason why she should not treat herself to a spontaneous, sexually charged adventure.

While waiting for Sam's X-ray results, Ursula pulled him into a deserted storage room. For the next half-hour, she pounded him senseless, leaving the small area in shambles and Sam with long, sweeping scratch marks covering his back. Which, of course, he treasured for months to come.

For the next three weeks, they met at bars and in motel rooms, as well as in the back of Ursula's utility van, where she had installed a comfortable mattress and several sex toys for her more mischievous moods. Their luscious rendezvouses were planned during lunch breaks—sometimes for just a quickie, other times for a much longer, more involved pounding between the sheets.

Ursula began calling him Stud Muffin Sam, or sometimes Sexy Sam. Or, after a few particularly steamy sessions, Slammin' Sam.

Mostly everyone else he knew simply called him Sam. Or just plain Hughes.

Hughes was the last name he heard before the lights went out. It was the name Ursula's husband uttered, followed by a long, heated string of enraged profanities, moments after the man crept into their bedroom, found Sam naked in bed with his trophy wife, and promptly blew him away with the satin silver .45 snub-nosed Smith & Wesson he had brought along for the special event.

Sam's thoughts slammed into utter chaos as he plunged into searing darkness when the horrifying explosion made by the hollowpoint slug slammed viciously into his brain.

Chapter 2

Sam's entire universe instantly turned black and sizzling hot.

He could easily tell he was falling. And falling. And as he fell, the blackness grew even blacker. And hotter.

Panic sliced through him. He was dead—he had to be. The deafening explosion. The horrendous fireball that had slammed into the back of his skull…

It had finally happened. Someone had killed him.

But that wasn't the important thing right now. What concerned him was the darkness enveloping him. The darkness and the fact that his fall continued. Most of all, he couldn't stop wondering why the darkness consistently grew hotter during his fall.

Just as his confusion grew unbearable, his fall ended abruptly. Before realizing what had happened, he landed with a sharp-sounding *splat!* on hot, muddy ground.

Slightly dazed, he pushed himself up into a sitting position. Squinting, he took careful inventory. Nothing felt broken, sprained, or twisted. He experienced no pain whatsoever. Everything seemed to be where and how it should be. As far as he could tell, he was not hurt.

This was baffling. Such a severe fall should have literally destroyed him, or at least turned him into a tangled pile of broken bones.

Then, in the midst of his mental chaos, the reality hit him.

If he were already dead, such a drop wouldn't have even mattered.

He *was* dead, wasn't he?

He had no idea. All he knew was that his back, side, and arms were covered in hot mud. He also noticed that this place really stunk. It smelled like fresh, pungent shit. No, worse. It took him only moments to determine its strong sulphurous reek.

Sulphur?

This could mean only one thing.

Slightly nauseous, he pushed the forbidden thought aside. At least, for now. There were more pressing issues to explore.

His main concerns were what had just happened and why he was no longer where he had been only moments ago.

The darkness surrounding him extended as far as the eye could see. The foul, steamy air drifting toward him brought about even more of a heavy sulfur stench. His eyes stung, watering so badly that he could no longer peer into the darkness.

He rubbed his eyes. At first, he didn't feel them. But after a few moments, the sulfur dissipated slightly, and his vision, though hazy, slowly returned.

This was something he could not understand. It made no sense. He couldn't even comprehend why his eyes stung in the first place. If he were dead, how could a pair of non-existent eyes have *any* feeling? And how could he possibly still have *hands* to rub them with? Would he continue to possess the senses he would need to adapt to this strange new environment?

Why did he have *anything* left, for that matter?

If he had indeed become a spirit, he *wouldn't* have much of anything. Everyone knew spirits were nothing more than masses of energy floating around in the atmosphere. Spirits, as he had read over the years, were merely hazy images of the dead seen only by mediums or other spirits.

What the hell had just happened to him?

Disregarding his stinging eyes, he forced himself to squint into the darkness. Soon the blackness cleared, transforming into a hazy red mist.

About twenty paces straight ahead, the mist faded. Just beyond it, a bizarre figure shimmered clearly.

A large throne surrounded by a wide circle of flaming coals appeared among the red mist. The throne seemed to be made of stone, glittering in the darkness as if painted or splashed with a thick gloss. A huge figure sat upon it. As Sam drew closer, it became clear that the figure was a naked female. At first he thought it was a statue. But when it moved, he realized the figure was that of an actual woman.

Her beautiful flawless face seemed reminiscent of a *Victoria's Secret* model. Her enormous dark blue eyes stayed dead steady on him, watching his every move. Her long, flowing, fiery red hair blew softly in the foul current of sizzling air, sliding across her yard-wide shoulders and down her arms.

Although she appeared to be twice his size, her features were in perfect proportion. A magnificent pair of perfect round breasts swelled proudly from her chest. Her forearms rested on the thick, flat arms of the throne. Occasionally she raised one of them to forcefully push her hair away from her face. Her long, shapely legs were crossed at the knee.

Her smooth golden flesh gleamed in the reddish mist. Her shoulders and arms were covered with rivulets of a thick, clear liquid. Streams of the stuff flowed between her breasts, continuing down her flat stomach.

Sam was both intrigued and aroused. If you liked your women enormous, beautiful, and huge breasted, this babe fit the bill perfectly. In the right circumstances, such a creature could be the answer to everyman's ultimate dream.

But this wasn't the right circumstance. Sam was almost certain he was dead. He didn't want to believe it, but his present surroundings—as well as what had just happened in Ursula's bedroom—suggested such a conclusion. After all, he'd been shot in the back of the head. When you're shot in the back of the head, your chances of survival aren't promising.

Then there was that somewhat minor detail of his falling into a hot, sulphurous pit. This was also something he couldn't exactly ignore. If this wasn't Hell, it could easily serve as a neighboring suburb.

So where did this leave him?

He wasn't certain, but he had the nagging feeling that the huge naked babe sitting on the throne just a few yards straight ahead could quite possibly be the one who would answer his questions.

Even if he was wrong, talking to her seemed likely to be the next logical step. However, the fact that she was gorgeous, naked, enormous, and covered in goo suggested that he should be extremely wary. Dark, frosty vibes emanated heavily from her gigantic orbs. Tendrils of flame flicked from her mouth and nostrils. And each time she lifted a naked arm to push back her hair, a thick cloud of almonds mixed with sweat—as well as the strong, unmistakable tang of sex—wafted his way.

He decided to reserve judgment. He had just arrived in a strange place and was now facing an extremely formidable female. It wouldn't be very bright to do or say anything stupid.

Just then, her arm extended. The claw-shaped, long-nailed index finger beckoned him closer.

Was this a good sign?

Sam had no idea. If this *were* Hell, he couldn't imagine any part of this exchange turning pleasant, or stress-free.

However, he had the strong feeling that he didn't have much choice. Her throne alone suggested to him that she was probably the one in charge of whatever kingdom this happened to be. Obeying her seemed the only sensible option. If he had learned anything in his short life, it was that you did whatever the in-charge told you to do. It didn't matter if the in-charge male or female; you made sure you did as you were told.

Nervous and bewildered, he took a few cautious steps closer. The mud covered his feet and ankles, making it difficult to move, but he forced himself. When he was about five feet away from the front line of burning coals, the heat had become unbearable. He backed up a foot or so and shielded his face with both arms.

The babe's index finger beckoned again. Sam took a tiny step forward and carefully lowered his arms.

She opened her mouth. Flames shot straight out, nearly reaching his flesh.

He was dead. He no longer consisted of flesh. So how could he feel the heat from a flame?

The fact remained. Whatever he still possessed, whatever he still was, continued to experience heat and discomfort. These sensations, whatever they were, appeared just as intense now as they would have been when he was alive. But he forced himself not to cry out. Holding everything in seemed a much more sensible career move. Although he knew nothing about where he was or who he now faced, something inside him strongly suggested that he should not anger this chick. Her stare made him think of a hungry wolf eyeing a trapped jackrabbit.

"What is your name?"

Her low-pitched, breathy voice, strong and full, echoed in the darkness. It was the sort of voice every man longs to hear in the bedroom.

"Samuel Hughes."

She tilted her head and watched him. He felt that she was studying him, as a vulture would eyeball a groundhog.

Sam forced out a pleasant smile. His smile usually worked with mortal females, so he decided to try it on this powerful, scary-looking lady. "You can call me Sam," he added, hoping she'd consider that as an offer of friendship.

She thought about that for a few moments. Then her eyes blazed, and her powerful voice filled the darkness once again. "I will call you Maggot."

Maggot. Wow. Really?

Although he didn't think the name fit him, he decided not to argue. He didn't think it would be very smart to correct this lady. At least, not now. He had learned long ago that it wasn't wise to get on the wrong side of a powerful woman. And since he had just seen this babe shoot flames with her mouth, he could tell she was someone he should really not mess with.

"What did you do up there?" she asked.

"Up where?" He had no idea what she was talking about.

"The mortal world--where else?"

He wondered why she wanted to know about his profession as a mailroom clerk. It wouldn't hurt to find out, would it? But somehow, the frivolous part of his character came right out, and he heard himself sounding like a total idiot. "Why do you want to know?"

More flames shot out of her mouth. "I *said*, what did you *do*?"

Sam realized right then that his humorous side would not work very well in this place. However, he still found himself clueless about her question. "About what?"

Her eyes filled the sockets. Her mouth opened, and thick tongues of flame shot out, singeing him and forcing him to his knees. He covered his head to shield himself from another blast.

Just then, he heard her groan. In a much softer voice, she said, "You truly *are* a maggot, Samuel Hughes."

Despite the scary circumstances, he decided to try asking her a question. He lowered his arms and straightened, nearly losing his balance on the soft mud. "Can you tell me something?"

"What would you like to know?" she asked, sounding bored.

"Why am I here?"

"What do you mean?"

"Why am I *here*, and not up *there*, in that other place?"

Her booming laughter shook the hot, clammy ground. "Because you are a maggot."

"Okay..." Maybe if he agreed with her, she'd tell him what he needed to know. "Is that why I'm here?"

"You are here because of your worth."

"My worth?"

"That, or lack of it. You will soon learn that this place contains only those that are dregs."

Dregs? Really? "I didn't think I was so bad."

"What good did you do up there?"

"Good?"

"Good. As opposed to bad, you idiot."

"Well, I..." It frustrated him that he couldn't think of anything good he had actually done.

"Did you help anyone? Save anyone's life? Redeem anyone?"

"I made dozens of women happy..."

"You didn't make anyone miserable? Sad? You destroyed no lives?"

"I broke up a ton of marriages and relationships—"

"That's *all* you did?"

Sam suddenly felt humiliated. And disgusted with himself.

A few moments later, she repeated her question: "So what did you do up there?"

"You mean, besides nailing women?"

Steam rose from her flesh. "Yes, Maggot, besides nailing women."

He shuddered. This babe was merciless. "I worked in the mail room at an insurance company."

"What else?"

"You mean in my spare time?"

Another flame—as well as a heavy blast of burnt almonds—brushed against him. He strongly suspected he wasn't getting on her good side.

"What did you do that made you what you were?"

16

Strange, her wanting to know about his character…

What was this? Some sort of job interview?

Sam had always considered his womanizing his strongest factor. He was married and divorced three times, had nailed more than two hundred women, and was caught cheating at least three dozen times. He always thought his insatiable sexual appetite explained why his relationships never lasted very long.

Even now he was thinking that if this babe wasn't so frightening and enormously powerful, he'd find a way to scale those long legs and help himself to a feast.

However, her sheer size—not to mention the flames leaping out of her mouth—strongly suggested that he might be much better off if he didn't tell her exactly what was on his mind. It wouldn't help his situation—not one bit. When you told the wrong woman how much you liked playing around, you were likely to get a firm knee to your groin. This had happened to him more often than he cared to remember.

The experience was something no man wishes to repeat.

"I guess I was always too obsessed with women and sex to consider anything else," he said finally.

She nodded. "I now understand why you were sent to me."

He hadn't figured that his obsession would send him to Hell for eternity.

"How many women, Maggot?" she asked curiously.

He shrugged. "I lost count a while ago."

"Give me an estimate."

He wondered why she needed one but decided not to stress the issue. "A couple of hundred, I guess."

She seemed to be thinking that one over. Judging by her expression, Sam figured this might actually be a good thing.

"How old were you when you started?"

"I was around twelve."

She remained silent for the longest time. She began studying him again.

While her eyes were focused on him, he watched how her long red hair slid across her breasts. Despite his confusion, he felt himself getting aroused.

She must have noticed it. Her eyes grew, and for a moment he thought he caught the beginnings of a smile touching her luscious lips.

"You're not a bad-looking creature, Maggot. A little baby-faced, perhaps. But you have possibilities. For a male."

Sam was pleased they were finally getting along. Maybe a little later, if things continued along their natural course, she might order him to climb those humongous legs. Size never mattered to him when it came to women. Most of the babes he had known were taller and larger than he was. This creature's melons and hot, wet flesh interested him much more than her being three or four feet taller than he was. He had learned long ago that men and women were the same height in bed.

"Thank you," he said. "Women usually take to me fairly quickly, although sometimes—"

"That was *not* a compliment. It was a *statement*. An *observation*. *Logic*. The discovery of a tool I might use at my discretion."

"Me? A *tool*?"

"I am the Demon of Lust," she said proudly. "Perhaps you have heard of me."

"I think I'd remember something like *that*..." It occurred to him that her wet, steamy flesh should have been self-explanatory.

"My name is Senyllia."

"I honestly don't think I've heard of--"

"It makes no difference. All I care about is how you might be of use to me. Tell me what you like to do."

"*Do*?"

"To *women*, you disgusting scrap of lizard slime!" The blast of flames shooting out of her mouth nearly knocked him over. "What do you like to do to them?"

He struggled to regain his balance. "The usual stuff."

"Such as...?"

"Well, first I take them out. Then, after a few drinks--"

"*Sex*, you hopeless dunderhead!" Another blistering blast whooshed by his face. "What kind of *sex*?"

19

He could tell right then that this babe didn't go in too much for small talk. He always wondered if she would approve of any sort of foreplay. "Every kind imaginable."

Her sensuous lips curled into a sort of sated smile. "Go on..."

"I like the rough stuff. Forcing them down."

"What else?"

"Rough. Hot. Steamy."

A glint of slobber touched her lower lip and inched down to her chin. Sam figured he had just hit pay-dirt.

"You are...a *rapist*?" she asked.

"Not exactly."

"What, exactly?"

"I like to manhandle them. To take charge."

Her smile deepened. Her huge breasts rose and fell. "Continue."

Sam found that he was getting seriously aroused. He always felt more alive when he talked about sex. He had no idea how he could feel more alive since he was now dead, but that was how this was turning out. He glanced down at himself and saw that he was even more aroused than he'd been just a minute ago.

But he wasn't too concerned about analyzing any of that right now. At present, the demon queen of hot, mind-blowing sex wanted to hear the gory details.

"I force them down—"

"And?"

"I spank them."

"Where?"

"Their asses. Their thighs. Their tits."

"With what?"

"A belt. A paddle."

"What else?"

"My hand."

Her smile stretched her cheeks. Slobber bubbled on her lower lip.

"Go on!"

As he continued, Senyllia's flesh glistened. A heavy jet of hot, thick juice splashed out, soaking him. He cringed, wiping the steaming fluid from his face. Some of it had covered his lips. Its taste was both sweet and bitter, tasting strongly of almonds. It turned him on even more.

Wow. The squirter of all squirters...

"Do not stop," she ordered, jagged flames spurting from her parted lips. "Go on!"

He went into further graphic detail, omitting nothing, telling her things he had never told anyone else.

More thick bursts of flame shot out from her. She writhed on her seat, her legs flailing, her hands clutching the arms of the throne. The almond scent thickened. The intense smell of her sex overwhelmed the sulfur reek.

When Sam had finished, she sat back and panted. Steam billowed up from her glowing flesh. Her matted hair covered most of her face, her breasts, and her shoulders. Her thighs and ankles were soaked. He half expected her to produce a cigarette out of thin air and light it with her tongue.

She shoved heavy knots of damp hair away from her face. In a tired voice she said, "*Now* I understand why you are here." She lowered her gaze briefly. Her eyes grew, and she nodded. "I also see that you're quite impressive for just an average-sized mortal male."

He looked down at himself and grinned. "Well, I don't like to brag, but--"

"Shut up."

Sam went silent.

She watched him closely. Her almond scent had thinned somewhat. Her soaked sex glittered like diamonds in the reddish fog. Her breasts rose as she took a breath. "As I have already told you, I am the demon of sexual desire. I have many pawns serving me, most of them female. I can always use a male who enjoys sex as much as I do. It has been many years since I have talked to a male who has aroused me at this level. I hope you will not disappoint."

Sam grinned. "No one has ever accused me of *that*…"

"Only time will tell, Sam Hughes…"

Sam Hughes. His real name. Not Maggot. He sighed in relief. Perhaps he had impressed her.

"Be assured," she said. "I am very demanding. And patience is not one of my virtues."

His gut told him not to comment on that one. "What would you want me to do?"

"Return to the world of mortals."

"You mean St. Cloud, Florida?"

She shrugged. "If that is where you wish to return to."

22

"But I'm dead. How can I do anything up there if I'm dead?"

"You shall be given back your mortal body before you depart from these chambers. You cannot act as my pawn without a mortal body. Any idiot should be able to figure that out."

"I guess you've got a valid point there. What about the nasty bullet hole in the back of my skull?"

"If you wish, we can leave it there."

"That really wouldn't be cool."

"Then why did you ask about it?"

"Just curious. I guess you know it's bound to attract a lot of attention."

"How so?"

"People tend to freak out if they see a fist-sized hole in the back of someone's head while they're still walking around."

She thought that over for a few moments. Then she looked him over. "You wouldn't want to wear a hat, would you?"

"If I'm going to have oodles and oodles of sex, I'll probably be forced to take it off."

"Females with strong sex drives usually don't care what the back of a man's head looks like, do they? I never did when I was mortal..."

He shrugged. "I kinda think they're different now."

"How so?"

"From what I've observed, the average female will freak or pass out if she sees a hole where there shouldn't be. I never liked having sex with an unconscious female."

23

She looked confused. "Really? With you, I would have thought otherwise."

"I honestly can't get off if the woman is just lying there like a rag doll. I tried it a few times when the babe was totally drunk, but it just didn't do much for me."

She nodded. "That will be taken care of, then."

"One other thing…"

A scowl. "And that is?"

"I'm wondering what will be different this time. I mean, up there."

"Since you are already dead, you will no longer have to worry about dying. And I shall give you certain powers."

The idea sounded interesting. "What sort of powers?"

"They will enable you to fulfill your tasks. You will understand once you return."

"Tasks?"

"Sex, lust, and uncontrollable desire."

This sounded too good to be true. There was probably some sort of catch she wasn't telling him about. Hell wasn't supposed to be a *cool* place, was it? He had always figured it was where all the evil or nasty souls went for eternity.

However, he didn't *feel* evil or nasty. Not at all. As a matter of fact, he felt damned good. He'd actually been sent to a spirit who got off on sex even more than he did. For him, this wasn't Hell at all, but that other place the religious fanatics talked about all the time. A place where all your dreams came true.

"Any other questions?" she asked.

"Just one…"

"Ask, then."

"What exactly do you expect me to do?"

"You have not already figured it out?"

"I'd like it if you told me outright."

She sighed. "Since you are obviously too stupid to think this out on your own… You are to seduce and violate every female you meet."

"That's *all* I have to do?"

"That is all."

He simply could not believe any of this. "That's something I can do with my eyes closed."

"As you already know, your witticisms are lost with me, Samuel Hughes."

"Sorry. I'll keep to the subject."

"Good. Do that or you will stay down here forever."

Sam shivered. "Don't worry. I'll make sure I nail every woman crossing my path."

"See that you do."

He wanted to laugh. And jump for joy. And maybe even do a cartwheel. "I feel like someone should pinch me."

She groaned. "I can shove a thunderbolt up your ass, if you wish."

"No, thank you. A pinch would do nicely."

She frowned. "Why would you require a pinch? Do you possess some other mental problem I should know about? Something other than monotonous witticisms and your obvious lack of mental acuity?"

He decided not to take issue with her observation. He didn't care for her thunderbolt idea, for one thing, and didn't want to say anything that could jeopardize his new mission in the mortal world, for another.

"I just can't stop thinking that I'm dreaming all this. I'll be okay once I get everything straight in my head."

"Your head is not the part I am concerned about."

"I understand."

"Understand this and you will know all this is necessary. I am content and happy as long as my subjects fulfill my purpose by wreaking havoc upon the earth."

"Havoc?"

"In my case, lust. I can exist as a powerful demon only if my subjects create constant lust in the mortal world. The more lust created, the more powerful I am. If my subjects fail me, I will lose my powers and turn back into the pathetic inferior I once was."

"How long have you been the Lust Demon?"

"For many centuries. Since I became a spirit, there has never been so much lust in the world. I am known as one of Hell's most powerful demons. This is why I choose my subjects wisely. And why my subjects never fail me. If you fail me, you will cease to exist, both spiritually and physically. In other words, if you do not obey my wishes, you will forfeit your immortality and return here to face my wrath."

"What will happen?" he asked uneasily.

"I will turn you into one of the maggots crawling around in the excrement on the filthy floor in the cellar of Hell, where Satan exists. Believe me, it is not a pleasant place."

"Bummer."

"I have warned you about your witticisms, Maggot."

"Uh, sorry..."

"I shall shove a giant fireball into that hole in the back of your head and retrieve it only after it has melted your pitiful brain into a tiny bubble of snot."

"Ouch."

"Do not disappoint me."

"I'll try not to."

"As long as you obey, you will enjoy the freedom of existing in the mortal world without fear of being caught or imprisoned. Or killed."

"Won't the ladies I'm wreaking havoc with object to all the havoc I'm going to wreak?"

"They will not remember you."

"Kind of a low blow for the old ego, but I guess that'll be okay."

"You wish to have an ego? Or would you rather sexually violate every female you come into contact with, without fear of discovery or reprisal?"

"You've got a point, I guess."

"This is how it shall be done."

"All righty, then. It sounds like a pretty nifty plan."

Her thick red brows arched, and her eyes bore into him. "I suspect you are mocking me, Samuel Hughes."

"I'm just trying to have a little--"

A wave of heat devoured him, sending a scorching sensation rushing down his limbs. He felt his body melting, shriveling into a searing husk of overly cooked meat while sinking into the ground. He could no longer feel his limbs. He also felt small and slimy as he slowly sunk into the hot mud. The ground reeked strongly of something disgusting. It covered his nose, eyes, and mouth. He began choking. His mind reeled and his head felt as if it were about to explode.

Then, just as he was about to fall into unconsciousness, the heat disappeared.

He stopped choking. The pressure in his head dissipated, and his vision returned. He quickly rose and found himself whole again. He looked down at himself. He was covered in mud as before, but at least he had survived. He turned to the lust demon, who continued frowning as she gazed back at him. "W-What happened?"

"I turned you into a sautéed slug."

"Why?"

"To demonstrate my power to you."

"Oh, I know you're powerful, baby--"

"*Lady Senyllia* to you, Maggot!" The flames roared outward. He cowered before her, using his arms to shield his face from a huge blast of smothering heat.

"Yes...uh...Lady Senyllia."

"Don't *ever* call me *baby* again!"

"No. Never."

"Not *ever!*"

"I promise."

"If there *is* a next time, I will turn you into something *much* worse than a sauteed slug."

He didn't even want to ask. "No problem, believe me."

"Good. Now get out of my sight. You have your instructions."

He reminded himself to hold back on the humor—at least until after he'd returned to the real world. "I'll honor them."

"See that you do. You will be amply rewarded."

That sounded promising. "How?"

"You shall have increased strength and stamina. And the power to seduce any woman of your choosing."

Sam was even more convinced than ever that this really was a supercool place. "That sounds terrific."

"Just live up to my expectations, or you will suffer the consequences."

He knew better than offer a witty comeback. He didn't want her doing that flame thing to his head. Or the face-in-the-mud thing. He also didn't enjoy being a slug--even for a second or two. "I won't disappoint you."

"I am glad. For a moment I was convinced you were nothing but a dick on two legs."

"I've been called that before."

29

"It is why we shall get along. But make sure you use your brain occasionally as well."

"One other thing--"

"We are finished."

"But—"

"Go forth and do my bidding, Samuel Hughes."

Her arm slowly raised, its index finger pointing directly at him. Tongues of flame shot out from it, encircling him. The heat was intense, excruciating. He opened his mouth to scream--

Everything disappeared.

The flames. The darkness. The reddish mist. The pit of Hell itself.

Even Lady Senyllia had vanished.

The blackness evaporated.

He opened his eyes.

He was lying beside Ursula.

Dark blood had soaked the pillow surrounding her head as well as the wall behind the headboard of the bed. She had been shot squarely in the forehead. She lay quite still, her eyes staring blankly at the ceiling.

Her husband lay face-down on the floor beside the bed, the back of his head also blown out. The huge, long-barreled gun he had used on Sam lay on the carpet inches from his outstretched hand.

What the hell happened?

Had Senyllia somehow changed the situation?

But how? Did she really have the powers to do something like this?

Didn't matter, did it?

The only thing that made sense right now was a hasty exit.

Chapter 3

Sam's head had cleared by the time he parked the Camaro in front of his apartment on Highway 192.

It was weird, coming back here after all that had happened, and even weirder that it had all happened so fast. A quick glance at the clock on Ursula's nightstand while he had picked up his clothes had said 10:08 A.M.

He remembered sneaking into her apartment a little before midnight. As far as he could recall, he had climbed into bed with Ursula, enjoyed some rough, mind-blowing sex for two hours, was shot by her husband an hour or so later, went down to Hell, made his arrangements with Senyllia, then came back up.

All in just eight or nine hours.

Incredible.

But did it really happen?

Was it a dream, perhaps? A hallucination?

Was it some weird nightmare brought on by the heavy drinking they had done before messing up the sheets?

Had Ursula slipped him something?

It was possible, wasn't it? Ursula could have given him something to totally mess up his head. She was a registered nurse and had access to all sorts of heavy-duty scripts. She knew exactly what meds did what.

But why would she give him anything that might affect his performance? A party animal since

32

her college days, Ursula went barhopping three nights a week like clockwork. She was a nymphomaniac and craved *sex*—not revenge or murder. She hadn't shown him anything but her wild, insatiable side since they'd known one another.

But something weird *had* happened.

Despite the fantastic feel of it all, the entire episode seemed totally *real*. Sharing drinks. The groping on the couch. The frenzied trip down the hall, to the bedroom. The furious shedding of clothing. More groping, then squeezing, licking, and sucking. Then two solid hours of bedroom acrobatics. Her husband sneaking into the apartment, bursting into the bedroom, cursing, then raising the gun.

The gunshot. The terrible, seething explosion in his head.

The fall.

The darkness.

The flaming coals.

The smell of almonds—of sulfur.

An enormous, beautiful, naked redhead sitting on a throne, breathing fire? Telling him she was the Lust Demon of Hell?

Maybe it *was* just a dream. He was back in his apartment, wasn't he? And his head was still in one piece, wasn't it? You couldn't possibly sustain a gunshot blast from a high-caliber gun at close range and keep your head in one piece.

He made a quick trip to the bathroom and stared at himself in the mirror. So far, so good…

33

From the front, that is…

You need to see the whole picture.

Suddenly uneasy, he picked up his hand-held mirror from the wicker basket on the counter and examined the back of his head.

No bullet hole. No blood.

His clothes were wrinkled and messed up, but there was no sign of blood or even mud on his clothes. They looked like they had been slept in, then tossed in a heap—nothing more.

He sniffed his hand.

The faint scent of almonds made him flinch.

Ursula? Or Senyllia?

He had known many women in his life. They all wore makeup and hairspray and nail polish and deodorant and powder and knew exactly where to apply everything for the best results. But despite anything different they might use, they all smelled basically the same.

Even so, he couldn't remember *any* of them giving off an almond scent.

So then, were the events of the previous night real?

Or did Ursula spill a bottle of vanilla extract on her arm in her kitchen while fixing their drinks?

She had made a batch of vodka martinis. This called for vodka, vermouth, shaved ice, and a lemon peel. There was no need whatsoever for vanilla extract.

And what about the mud?

He had obviously fallen into soft, hot mud. And when he was changed into a charburoiled slug by the

34

Lust Demon, he was completely submerged in the stuff.

Why weren't his clothes covered with it?

That was simple. His clothes hadn't gone anywhere. They had spent the last ten hours on the floor in Ursula's bedroom.

Remember how your dick had become swollen when you were telling Senyllia about your escapades? And how she clearly noticed it?

She couldn't have seen it so clearly if you'd been wearing clothes, right?

That seemed to make perfect sense. His spiritual form had made the trip—*not* his clothes.

This all seemed to make some sort of sense, but he couldn't help wondering about the natural logic of the previous events.

No bullet hole. No blood.

And what about the gunshot? The searing, blistering pain? The total darkness? The fall?

There *had* to have been a gun. He had heard the blast, felt it, tasted its bitterness as it destroyed his skull.

Then he remembered. He had seen it.

It was lying on the floor, not far from her husband's dead body. And Ursula was lying in the bed, the bullet hole in her forehead—as well as the blood spatter on the wall above the bed—clear evidence of what had happened.

The most important detail bugging him was the fact that he was sitting in his car outside his apartment.

How the hell did he manage to escape the wrath of Ursula's husband while the enraged man was pointing a gun at his—

Senyllia. It had to be. She was powerful— wasn't she? You would *have* to be powerful to be the Lust Demon of Hell, wouldn't you? Of *course* she was powerful. After all, she had turned him into a slug without any effort whatsoever.

She called him her "subject." This meant she owned him. This also meant that he was her property and that she would make it where nothing would interfere with his mission to do her "bidding."

Senyllia was indeed calling the shots. *She* had done all this. She had made it where he had escaped the gun, the devastating shot to the back of his skull, the furious husband—the works.

And lastly, she had made it where he was able to dress, walk out to his car, and come back home. Unscathed. And with the back of his head intact.

Incredible.

A glance at the living room clock told him he had a few hours until he was scheduled to show up for work. Until then, he could easily find out if the meeting with the Lust Demon had indeed happened.

Senyllia had something about giving him powers. She didn't say what sort of powers they'd be. She hadn't even said when these powers would manifest themselves. But she did mention that he wouldn't have to worry about being caught or imprisoned. Or killed.

And what was his mission?

"Seduce and violate every female you meet…"

What a deal. It sounded too good to be true.

He decided to do a little sniffing around at Walmart. All sorts of babes shopped there. It would be the perfect place to find out if he really had been given special powers.

But before he did anything, he needed a shower. The almond scent was strong; it might arouse suspicion in a crowded store.

He peeled off his clothes and dropped them in a heap on the bathroom floor. After his shower, he put on fresh clothes, splashed his cheeks with Stetson, went out, and got into the Camaro.

Chapter 4

Walmart was already somewhat busy by the time Sam eased into the half-filled lot a few minutes after eleven.

Inside, female shoppers pushed carts loaded with purchases up and down the aisles. Many hauled small kids around and wore loose, ill-fitting clothing. Sam spotted a couple of desirable prospects but decided to take his time and be selective. If what he had experienced the previous night had indeed happened as he remembered, he had no intention of being arrested for assault, losing his job, and spending months in jail.

For the next half hour, he pushed his cart down the aisle, occasionally tossing in an item to give the store cameras the illusion that he was an actual shopper. The store filled gradually, mostly people stopping by on their lunch break.

It was nearly twelve o'clock when the perfect specimen entered the store. In her mid- or late twenties, the babe was tall and slender, and dressed in a simple copper blouse, black skirt, and high-heeled black pumps. Her thick black hair, sparkling in the store lighting, fell a couple of inches below her shoulders. Her tan told him she was a local. Her dark-brown leather handbag and gold bracelets conveyed the unmistakable message that she had good taste as well as money to spend.

She pushed her cart down the aisle toward Ladies' Wear, turning right and disappearing

38

amongst the racks of hanging blouses and slacks. Halfway down the aisle, she began riffling through a section of pricey long-sleeve blouses.

Sam considered this the perfect setup. She was hidden from view of the main area and preoccupied, which made her vulnerable. To make things even more convenient, the dressing rooms were just ten feet straight ahead. If he could follow her into one of the rooms, he would find out very quickly if he really had gone to Hell, engaged in a conversation with the Demon Queen of Lust, and was given special powers.

Sam left his cart between two bargain bins of open-toed sandals and discount purses and slipped down the aisle behind her.

So far, so good. The babe was still immersed in her hunt for the perfect blouse and didn't even turn around as he drew nearer.

Most people feel safe in a store like Walmart.

She was reaching for something from the top rack when he walked up to her. Hearing his footsteps, she turned around and glanced at him. He expected her to say something, gasp, or even scream. She merely gawked at him, her large dark eyes taking him in.

Silence.

It was an awkward moment. The fear of arrest sliced through him again. Something just didn't *feel* right. Sam's first reaction was to smile, turn around, and quietly walk away. He obviously *hadn't* gone to Hell. He had no doubt driven to Ursula's apartment and spent half the night with her. Then, once exhaustion had set in, he fell asleep and was dozing soundly while her husband burst in, shot her, then turned the gun on himself.

It sounded weird and highly unlikely but offered a definite possibility.

At least, it seemed more of a possibility than what he had been thinking.

The reason this babe wasn't screaming could be because she didn't consider him a serious threat. It was also possible that, like most of the other women he had known in his life, she was attracted to his big blue eyes.

This lady sure was a looker—and with a hot little body. But he knew better than try something in a busy place like Walmart.

Just smile politely, turn around, and leave this babe alone…

Just then, her eyes glazed over. Then lowered.

She moved closer, lowered her left arm, and began rubbing him. Her right arm came up and encircled his neck. Before he could react, her lips mashed onto his.

She backed up slowly, pulling him by the neck, her mouth still pressed to his. He let her lead him, and in seconds they had gone into the dressing room. She let go of his neck and slammed the door shut. Her other hand quickly dropped to her side. Her lips and tongue continued kissing him as she hiked up her skirt.

He had never encountered something this exciting before. The girls he had known had demanded conversation—at least to tell him their name or to ask his—before engaging in heavy foreplay. Not one of them had *ever* done anything like this.

This was seriously strange.

And utterly fantastic.

She pulled away. Her hot breath smothered his face. Her lavender scent enveloped him. "You want more of this?" she whispered, her mouth just inches from his.

"Uh, yeah…"

Her lips covered his own, sending a tremor charging down his spine. Her eyes watched him as she pushed down her panties. "Latch the door," she whispered.

He did as she said.

She tossed her panties onto the wooden bench, reached out, and clumsily unbuckled his belt. She paused briefly. "I really want this," she whispered, her gaze lowered, focused on him.

He helped her by pushing down his trousers.

She dropped to her knees. He reached down and grabbed her hair. She moaned. He closed his eyes and enjoyed the delicious moment.

Long before he wanted her to stop what she was doing, she was standing again, her teeth nibbling his lower lip. "Now I really want *this*," she whispered, her hot breath in his face. "Right *now!*"

She bent over. The smooth round globes of her ass twitched as she bent forward and rested her hands on her knees. "Do it to me, baby," she whispered hoarsely.

"Want me to hurt you?"

41

"Hurt me, baby."

He pushed her into the corner, clamped a hand over her mouth, and swatted her. She gasped, her hot breath and wet lips instantly heating up his palm.

"Like that?" he whispered close to her ear.

She moaned, nodding eagerly. He swatted her again. She gasped and shuddered. A whiff of her perfume and her lavender scent, so close to his face, sent even more waves of desire billowing through him.

He pulled his hand away from her mouth and cupped his hands over her tits. "These are nice," he whispered, his mouth only an inch from hers. "Juicy. Hot."

"Squeeze them."

He squeezed them and she groaned.

"Harder."

He squeezed harder. Her eyes grew, and she gasped.

He put his hand over her mouth again. He shoved his index finger between her lips and blew in her ear, making her shudder as she nibbled on his finger.

Her chest heaved. "Do me," she whispered, her breath smothering his face. "Now. *Please...*" A weak moan trickled from her nostrils.

It was time.

***

What seemed an eternity later, Sam helped her sit on the wooden bench. She sat slumped over, her head down, her hair hiding her face and shoulders.

42

As she sat there, heaving, he pulled up his trousers. Then he picked up her panties and helped slide them back up to her knees. She stood up just long enough to help him pull them up the rest of the way. Then she sat back down and slumped on the bench.

He kissed the top of her head and opened the door.

Her head was still lowered when he left the room.

Slightly bewildered, he made his way toward Electronics.

It seemed evident that he had indeed gone to Hell and made some sort of deal with the Lust Demon. What had just happened defied any other explanation. It didn't seem logical that a normal guy could just look at a strange woman in a crowded store, then stand idly by while she approached him, yanked him into the nearest dressing room, dropped to her knees, and immediately turned into his dream whore.

It had been much too easy. Going by her refined, attractive appearance, he could see that she was intelligent. She most likely ran her own business or worked as someone's executive assistant. She just didn't seem the type to grab a stranger at first glance, talk dirty to him, drag him into a dressing room, then open her thighs.

Judging by what had just transpired, Sam concluded that he *had* been given unusual powers.

This was fantastic. The more he thought of it, the more he realized just how lucky he had been, getting blown away by Ursula's jealous husband.

43

His descent into Hell and his meeting with Senyllia had turned his grisly murder into something any sex-loving man with enough working brain cells would consider the ultimate nirvana.

But even so, he still wasn't quite sure about all this. There had to be one sure way to find out if Senyllia had been speaking the truth when she told him he wouldn't have to worry about getting into trouble.

Like it or not, he had to find out.

He had reached the Bargain Movies Bin when he saw the brunette coming out of Ladies' Wear, her hair still a mess, her clothing rumpled. Her expression was blank and a little dazed as she shuffled in his direction.

When she was about ten steps away, he slipped between the bargain bins and cut in front of her.

"Hi." He gave her a friendly wave.

It was kind of unnerving, talking to a total stranger you had just had sex with, but he had to find out about all this.

She merely glanced at him. The blankness in her eyes revealed nothing.

Something was different. Something--

Her bag. She wasn't carrying her bag.

She had left it with her cart in Ladies' Wear.

In normal circumstances, a woman would not leave her handbag anywhere—especially a top-of-the-line leather job like the one she had brought with her. A woman carried everything in her bag—makeup, wallet, money, credit cards, cell phone, photos. Also, pepper spray and, in some cases, a small handgun. Even if she had been distracted enough to walk away from her cart, she wouldn't have forgotten her bag.

The only way a woman would leave her bag is if she were dazed, suffering from amnesia, or kidnapped.

Their spontaneous sexual frenzy had obviously done a major number on her head. She not only had forgotten her handbag, she also didn't recognize him.

She kept on walking.

He couldn't let her go like this.

"Excuse me."

She stopped walking and turned. "Yes?" She pushed some stray knots of hair away from her face.

"I couldn't help noticing. Your handbag."

"Pardon me?"

"I saw you pushing a cart into Ladies' Wear. I assume your bag's still in the cart."

She looked down at herself, giving him the impression that she had just awakened from a deep sleep. She checked her hands, then her shoulder, possibly to verify that her bag wasn't hanging from its strap. Then she looked at him and frowned. She appeared very confused.

"That *is* your cart back there, isn't it?"

"My *God!*" She rushed back to Ladies' Wear and disappeared behind the racks.

He followed her.

She was picking up her bag and rummaging through it when he walked over. "Everything there?"

She spun around. Seeing him, she shuddered. Then, as an afterthought, she looked around—as if to get her bearings. "I…don't *know*. Something really weird just happened…"

"Can I help?"

"No. Yes. I…don't *know*." She shoved a hand roughly through her hair. "I…must be working too hard. My mind…it's gone totally blank!"

"Mine does that, too, sometimes."

"But this…this is really *creepy*." She shivered. "I could've sworn I just had a—" She stopped and stared at him. Her eyes immediately grew blank. They were just about to lower to his crotch when he remembered what had been going on.

The stare.

That *had* to be it. Nothing else made sense. It no doubt had something to do with the powers Senyllia had given him. The last time their eyes had locked on to one another, this woman lowered her eyes to his groin area and instantly turned into his sex slave.

Nope. I can't put her through this again…

Sam quickly turned away. He hoped that all she needed was a few seconds to snap out of it. To break the connection.

When he looked at her again, she blushed and pushed her hair away from her face. "Like I said, I must be working too hard."

"Are you sure you're all right?"

"No. Thanks. Really."

"What *do* you remember?" To avoid her eyes, he shifted his attention to her handbag, then to one of the bargain bins behind her. Then he transferred his attentions to her hair. It badly needed a quick comb, but she would have to discover that for herself.

"I honestly don't know. I remember looking through the blouse rack. Then something...something just... I guess my mind just blanked out, like I said. I woke up in one of the dressing rooms, but I don't exactly remember going in there..." She reddened. He figured she was wondering why her skirt was off and her panties were on the bench beside her.

"Maybe you were deep in thought when you took something in there and—"

"That's just it. I didn't see anything hanging from the hook or lying on the bench. I obviously didn't take *anything* in there. So why did I even go *in* there?"

He wanted to smile. Senyllia had done quite a job. She told him they wouldn't remember him, but he thought she was only toying with him.

How could that be possible? How could a woman have sex with you, then forget you immediately after?

But it was true. Otherwise, this girl would have scratched his eyes out the instant she saw him again.

Senyllia *hadn't* been toying with him. She *was* telling him the truth. When she said he wouldn't have to worry about getting into trouble, she meant it.

"I could walk you back to your car," he suggested.

"No. Really. I'm fine now. Thanks."

"No problem."

She didn't move. She was staring again.

He quickly turned away.

It was time to walk away and let this woman live the rest of her life. He waved and hurried down the aisle. When he thought it was safe, he glanced behind him.

Her bag clutched tightly to her side, she rushed toward the front entrance.

He watched to see if she would turn around.

She didn't.

He had actually died, gone to Hell, and come back in a much better position than ever before. He had the power to do things any man in his right mind could only dream about.

He had also learned something no one living would ever be able to comprehend.

Hell was actually *Heaven* for guys like him.

Chapter 5

Whistling in her typical off-key manner, Sheila Schmidt hovered over the cluttered table in her tight jeans and bright-red V-necked blouse, sorting the thick stacks of afternoon mail.

Sam came in at a few minutes before four, went right over to his desk, and logged on.

Sheila worked from eight to five. She came into the mailroom promptly when the company opened its doors and left about an hour after Sam arrived for his four-to-twelve.

Sheila was a hot-blooded forty-two with large tits and a full round ass. She had made it known from the day Sam started working at Stram/Loc/Headler Computer Distribution Services over a year ago that he was not her type. Sheila liked her men tall, broad-shouldered, and rough-looking. She also preferred beards and tattoos. Or at least a sexy mustache and a tasty ear stud. Tongue studs were also a plus. So were shaved heads and Mohawks. She had also mentioned a penchant for scars—especially in the "right area."

It was easy to see why Sam didn't interest her.

This suited him just fine. Sheila wasn't exactly Sam's type, either. Besides, he had never wanted to get involved with a co-worker. It would cause all sorts of complications and stress, and usually caused one—or both—of the people involved to quit or switch departments. Sheila also had an extensive track record. She had been divorced four times, had five kids, and had never really learned how or when to keep her mouth shut—all important factors that had always been very important to Sam in his selection of suitable females.

She gave him her usual disparaging stare the moment he walked in, her large green eyes on him as he sat down at his computer.

He was accustomed to her cold stares. Most of the time he just ignored her. However, today somehow proved different. Since his recent experience at Walmart, he knew full well that he would have to be especially careful in his dealings with women. And since Sheila was a high-spirited, highly sexed female, she would also have to be approached with utmost caution.

He still found it difficult to believe that he now possessed special powers, and that all he had to do to attract a woman was stare at her in a certain manner.

It all seemed so incredible.

He forced himself to stop thinking about it. Since he was now at work, he should concentrate on his job. But each time he was convinced his mind had returned to the work mode, the image of the brunette in the Walmart dressing room drifted back, shattering all former thoughts. He felt himself getting aroused once again and began squirming uncomfortably in his chair.

He knew damned well that he had better do something to keep from being noticed. Sheila was still staring at him. He didn't want to get up from his chair when the swelling in his jeans had become so obvious.

He took his mind off the issue by checking his email and deleting his scam messages. In a little while, he would start his tracking research before sorting the afternoon incoming, collecting it, itemizing and separating it, then pushing it through the maze of cubes using the company mail cart.

His mind immediately began wandering again, and in no time, the image of Senyllia dominated his thoughts. A moment later, the brunette popped up yet again. And before he knew it, the picture screen in his head showed Ursula lying dead in her own bed, her dead husband sprawled on the floor a couple of feet away.

He reminded himself that he was also dead. However, he had made a deal with a demon. And as long as he continued doing work for her, his existence as a mortal was assured.

He wondered how many other dead people were also wandering around. He had seen lots and lots of idiots in his thirty-two years. They ambled around like zombies. Were they also dead? Or was it because they hadn't found a demon that had chosen them and given them powers?

He began wondering if Ursula or her husband had met a similar demon after making their plunge.

I'm thinking too much about this seriously weird shit and it'll drive me crazy if I don't stop.

Ten minutes later, he finally managed to clear out his queue. He looked down at himself before he rose from the chair. It was safe to stand. Sighing in relief, he got up and went to grab some coffee from the station in the corner of their area.

Sheila was still watching him.

"Problem?"

She sauntered over and stopped about a foot short. Her breasts, as usual, nearly touched him. "You all right?"

He had always wanted to ask why she got so close to a guy she wasn't interested in. He decided not to. It might give her the impression he might be interested. Besides, he really didn't want to know. He figured it was one of the many things women did unconsciously to torment men.

"Why?" he asked.

She shrugged. "You're acting...well, different."

His first impulse was to just shake his head—or shrug—and walk away. He decided there was no need. She couldn't possibly know or see anything. She was just being her usual nosy self.

He added some sugar to his coffee. "Different how?" he asked casually.

She looked him up and down. "Can't put my finger on it."

He took the steaming cup back to his desk. "When your finger finds whatever it's looking for, you can just keep it to yourself."

She followed. When he turned, he caught her staring at his crotch. He suddenly noticed that her eyes had already glazed over.

Then it dawned on him. He turned away quickly, hoping it wasn't too late.

52

"C'mere."

"I've got my tracking--"

She grabbed him by the belt buckle and pulled him toward her. He tried resisting, but she was much stronger than he thought. "What the hell do you think you're--"

"The Supply Room." Her voice was low and gruff. "*Now!*"

"But--"

"I said *now!*"

Sheila backed up to the door, opened it with one hand, glanced to her right to see that no one was coming in, then pulled him in after her and slammed the door.

His mind reeled as he watched her click the lock on the door. "Whatever you have in mind is not very bright, you know."

"Shuddup."

"We're on company property."

"Shuddup." She pushed him onto one of the tables, where piles of computer paper boxes reached halfway to the ceiling. She bent him over the table, pulled down his trousers and grabbed him with both hands. "Didn't think you'd be this big," she whispered, her eyes enormous.

"It's not something I normally tell...everyone," he said through clenched teeth.

"We'll keep it to ourselves, then."

He closed his eyes and cursed himself for not seeing this coming. He would definitely have to be doubly careful who he stared at from now on. He wanted to apply the stare thing to a woman he

53

wanted to have sex with. No one else. And certainly no one like Sheila.

This was all wrong. He just hoped Sheila's mind would go blank when she was finished.

The powers Senyllia had given him quite possibly had something to do with that flame she had wrapped around him just before sending him back to the land of the living. It was the only thing that made sense.

The flame had somehow made him irresistible.

Not a bad thing, normally. No self-respecting man on earth would object to such a tremendous change in his physical chemistry.

But he would have to make certain adjustments. He needed to be out in the mailroom right now, tracking and sorting. He didn't need to be lying on a table in the Supply Room, watching Sheila doing such incredibly painful and very satisfying things to him.

"I really don't think this is a good idea," he whispered uneasily.

"Shuddup."

"We'll get caught if anyone--"

"I said shut *up!*"

He lay back and let her work.

Five minutes later, he climaxed violently.

Eyes closed, he lay still, waiting for his heart to return to normal.

Moments later, the door opened, then closed. Panicking, he jumped up and frantically pulled up his pants.

He was alone in the big, cluttered room.

Sheila had already left.

**

Sheila was sorting mail when he came back. She had her radio on soft and was humming along with her idol, Shania Twain.

"What were you doing in there?" she asked without looking up.

Thank God she doesn't remember...

"Looking for envelopes." He went back to his desk and picked up his coffee cup. It had gone cold.

"You've got some on your desk."

"Guess I didn't notice."

"They're right there, in front of your console."

"How about that? They really are right there. In front of my nose all along!"

"You really are weird, ya know..."

"I know, but my mother didn't tell me about it until I was out on my own."

Sheila said nothing.

Her hair and a small portion of her right cheek gleamed in the overhead lighting with drops of his sperm. He forced himself not to smile and wondered if he should say anything. He didn't want to set her off. Sheila had a short fuse and could turn into a frightening wildcat when angered.

"Wearing your hair different?" he asked.

"Been too busy to comb it." She reached up and pushed it away from her face. She must have felt something on her cheek. She stared dumbly at it, wiped her hand on her jeans, and went back to work.

55

Five minutes later, she put the stack in the bin and went to clock out. "Guess I'll be leaving now." She put her timecard back in its slot.

"Have a good weekend."

"Maybe I'll get lucky." She opened the door and hurried through.

"You just were," he mumbled.

She stuck her head through the opening. "Whazzat?"

"Just clearing my throat."

"Yep. Weird, all right."

The door slammed shut.

Sam went back to his sorting. He managed to sift through half a stack before something caught his attention in the main office area.

Outside the mailroom window, Tonya, one of the dynamite supervisors on the floor, sashayed down the aisle. She glanced in his direction. Sam immediately turned away. It was much too soon to go at it again, even with a babe who looked like Tonya. He picked up his stapler and placed it in a drawer. Then he turned back to the window. Tonya had already disappeared in her cube.

Satisfied no more surprises awaited him, he poured a fresh cup of coffee, went back to his table, and tried concentrating on his job.

Chapter 6

At midnight, the parking lot was nearly deserted. The few remaining vehicles belonged to the skeleton crew from the computer room and two security guards.

Sam suddenly realized he was tired. He also discovered that he was more tired than usual. He knew right off that he shouldn't be surprised. After all, he had had a very busy day. In less than twenty-four hours, he'd been through more than any normal man should endure in a lifetime. He was shot and killed. He was then sent to Hell. Upon his return, he engaged in heavy sexual acrobatics with a good-looking brunette in Walmart as well as some impressive action from Sheila Schmidt in the Supply Room.

But after further rationalization, he didn't think he should be so tired. From what Senyllia had told him, the best way to increase his strength and stamina was to nail as many women as possible.

He suddenly realized that he should probably have another go at it with another babe.

It was, after all, Friday night. After a couple of drinks and another sexual encounter, he'd no doubt feel much better.

He started up the Camaro, pulled out of the lot, and headed east, toward St. Cloud.

***

Only a few vacant spaces remained amongst the long row of vehicles parked in front of the Western Trail Bar & Grill.

The one-story building, fronted with faux logs fashioned to resemble a modern-day cabin, sat in a grove of trees about a mile or so west of St. Cloud and one block south of 192. Directly above the front entrance, a wagon wheel painted bright-red and bolted to the shingle roof could be seen clearly from the main drag. Hitching posts fronted the place. The life-size statue of an obese bay Quarter Horse graced a large square concrete slab at the western end of the building.

As Sam parked between two black Dodge pickups smeared with caked mud and covered with NRA stickers, he wondered how many drunken cowboys had tried sitting on the horse.

Inside the long, semi-dark room, the juke bounced happily with Alan Jackson singing about his classic Mercury. Happy customers yucked it up at tables and at the bar. On the dance floor, a dozen or so half-drunk couples struggled to stay on their feet while keeping with the beat.

Sam took a stool at the end of the bar. Six stools down, three hookers tried their best to attract clients. Two of them appeared to be at least forty, the third slightly younger. Sam guessed that their loose, heavily tattooed flesh turned off the most promising prospects. The platinum blonde turned his way and smiled. So did the redhead beside her. He was careful not to look directly at them. He wasn't in the mood for a pro. Pros turned sex into a transaction—a cold, obligatory chore best done quickly and efficiently. Sam had never paid for sex in his entire life.

After ordering a Manhattan from the tall, broad-shouldered barman, he sat back and watched a few of the guys making out with their female companions at the tables.

His drink came. It was strong. He downed half of it, then went back to watching everyone.

He finished his drink a few minutes later and ordered another. Exhaustion began creeping into his limbs again. More residual fatigue from his trip to the bowels of the earth? Or was it something else? He was thirty-two, for God's sake. He wasn't accustomed to being so tired. Before his descent, he could go well into the night before fatigue set in.

What was different?

He tried remembering everything Senyllia had told him. And what he had told Senyllia. According to their arrangement, he would nail every woman crossing his path. This pleased her. Lust made her more powerful, and any failure on his part in this endeavor would mean his death, both spiritually and physically. His immortality would be forfeited, and he would quickly return to Hell to face her wrath.

She also threatened to turn him into a maggot. And, of course, shove a giant fireball into his head.

He saw no problem with this strange arrangement. He would have increased strength and stamina. And, of course, the power to seduce any woman of his choosing. But if he wasn't doing what

Senyllia expected of him, he would most suffer the consequences.

What were *they*?

This sudden, mysterious fatigue?

Something worse?

He had seen ancient reruns of *Twilight Zone* episodes when he was younger. If this situation paralleled a *Twilight Zone* script, he could suffer the opposite of whatever power Senyllia had given him.

From what he suspected, the opposite of strength and stamina was weakness and frailty.

He told himself that he was worrying about nothing. He hadn't messed up. He had already made it with two women in just twelve hours. Wasn't that enough?

No one in his right mind could argue with *that* sort of logic.

But how could he explain this strange fatigue?

If it indeed *was* the result of not engaging in enough lust, how often did Senyllia expect him to keep this up?

He had seen her, talked to her. He had also seen samples of her power, her wrath. She was the real deal. The epitome of badass. The Ball-Buster Supreme. She *expected* him to keep up the pace and would not hesitate to haul him back down if she wasn't satisfied with his results.

He finished his drink, then scoured the place for a suitable victim.

Every decent female appeared to be with someone.

Frustrated, he got up, crossed the room, and wandered down the hall marked *COWBOYS*. He thought it would be wise to wait around until he spotted someone interesting, then whisk her away and nail her in one of the stalls. His plan might prove tricky if the bathroom were crowded, but he would have to struggle through such an obstacle. His brief encounter with Senyllia strongly suggested that he didn't have the luxury of waiting too long for the perfect opportunity.

He suspected he had better find someone fast.

As Senyllia had already told him, she was not the most patient of spirits.

***

Halfway down the dimly lit hall, Sam leaned against the paneled wall near the three payphones. He didn't want anyone thinking he was waiting to pounce on any female on her way to or coming out of the ladies' room and consulted his watch whenever someone passed. But he really was on the lookout for a suitable prospect.

After about ten minutes, a skinny blonde with silicone jugs and pouty lips staggered out of the ladies' room. She wore a skimpy black tee shirt at least three inches shy of her navel, frayed jeans that looked like they had been sprayed on, and open-toed white pumps. Glitter highlighted her hair, which sparkled in the small overhead light. A diamond stud pierced her left cheek. A larger one sat just above her right nostril, and a silver ring embellished each painted brow. He suspected she

61

also wore a tongue stud. She smiled at him as she passed, then disappeared around the corner.

He followed and soon discovered that she was rushing straight for the back door at the end of the hall, which led to the gravel lot.

Suddenly intrigued, he stayed just a few yards behind her as she crossed the rear lot leading to the woods just beyond the property.

She staggered down the long line of parked vehicles, moving unsteadily, nearly losing her footing on the uneven ground but correcting her balance against the hood of an ancient TransAm. Once she reached the end of the row, she stopped beside a battered two-tone Ford pickup and shoved a tiny hand down the front pocket of her tight jeans.

Sam walked over just as she unlocked and opened the driver's door. "Hi."

She smiled. "You're the cute guy standing outside the shitter."

"I've been called much worse."

A sloppy giggle. "You really are cute."

"I think you already covered that."

"Just wanted to make sure ya—" Her light-blue eyes glazed over. Her face lowered.

Her nearness and her sweet smell perked him right up. She was a hot, good-looking babe. The glaze in her eyes had coaxed him nearly fully erect in just seconds.

She reached down and covered his crotch. "Mmmm," she whispered, breathing a heavy cloud of gin in his face. "Lotsa hot and heavy stuff goin' on down there."

"You've got a way with words."

A giggle. "I been told that before."

He suspected she was lying but realized he could be underestimating her. Knowing how complex society was nowadays, he guessed she could be the head of a software company—or even a lawyer—when she was all cleaned up and sober. "I'll bet."

Another giggle. "Everybody says my mouth's the best thing about me."

Now he understood. "I'll have to take their word for it."

She blinked and suddenly looked confused. "You don't wanna find out for yourself?"

"Thought you'd never ask."

She grinned stupidly.

"You here alone tonight?"

Her grin vanished. "Stupid old man told me to get fucked."

"You really should do what your elder says."

"Huh?"

"You didn't quite get that, did you?"

Her grin returned. "Somethin' tells me I'm about to…"

"You've got good instincts."

Still grinning, she moved closer. "Whaddya have in mind?"

"I'd like to make sure you do what your old man said. Don't want you to get in trouble, do we?"

"Baby, you're talkin' at me really weird."

"What I'm trying to say, I guess, is that I'd like to find out if everyone's right."

63

"About what?"

"Your mouth."

She moved even closer and pushed another heavy cloud of gin in his face. "Get in."

"The truck?"

She laughed loudly. "You really *are* cute!" She opened her door and jumped up onto the running board. He circled the truck and opened the passenger door while she slid in behind the wheel and slammed her door.

"I'm just a smidge wasted," she said, squirming into a comfortable position. "But I can still get the job done."

He could feel his jeans getting tighter. "You've already done a damned good job by sheer innuendo."

She blinked. "Cher did *what* in your window?"

"Never mind." Her last remark told him he had been way off base with his thoughts of her being a lawyer or the head of a software company.

"Ya know something, baby? You talk kinda snooty, but ya sure do turn me on." She slid over and began tugging at his belt. Her hands worked furiously.

She acted like she hadn't done this in a while.

"How long has it been?"

She stopped tugging. "Since what?"

"Since you got laid."

She went back to working on his belt. Then she stopped for a moment. She seemed to be thinking it over. "At least an hour. Maybe two."

"For a minute I was worried you might've forgot where everything is."

"Don't worry about *that*, baby." She got his pants opened and pulled down enough to expose his swollen organ. "Wow... *Nice!*"

He took a deep breath and tried focusing on something that had been bothering him. "This guy of yours," he managed.

She raised her eyes but didn't let go of him. "Hmmm?"

He gritted his teeth. "The guy...who told you...to fuck yourself."

She raised her head and frowned. "Fuck him."

Apparently they had broken up. Good deal.

He settled back in his seat and closed his eyes. It wouldn't be long now. The last remnants of his fatigue had already vanished.

His door suddenly squealed open.

A huge, leather-clad torso reeking of beer and cigarettes filled the doorway less than three feet away.

Sam found himself staring at a large silver belt buckle, leather vest, hairy chest, and two large muscular arms. A black leather do-rag tightly wrapped around the top of the man's head completed the wild biker ensemble. The man's heavily bearded face snarled like a wolf about to attack.

"What the fuck ya think you doin', sumbitch?"

Despite the obvious menace facing him, Sam found that he wasn't frightened. He was, however, irritated by the sudden intrusion. His plans for the evening had just blown up in his face.

Under normal circumstances, he would have made tracks. He was a lover. He had never been a fighter and never wanted to be.

But things were different now. He no longer had to worry about the same threats that concerned him when he was alive. He had died and gone to Hell. What could possibly happen that would make the situation worse? Even if this guy was as tough as he looked, Sam knew he was in no danger of being killed.

How could you kill someone who was already dead?

All these factors prevented him from being scared. And the fact that he was dead had made Sam much more arrogant than he had ever been in his mortal life.

"What's it look like, Einstein?" he heard himself saying. "Do the math. You just interrupted one super-fine blow job—"

"You stupid fuck!" The huge, gnarled hands shot outward, grabbing the front of Sam's shirt. Sam was yanked out of the truck, pulled roughly to the side, and slammed to the hard gravel.

The shock of the gravel crunching into his shoulder blades and the back of his head snapped him out of it. The intense pain took him completely by surprise. This shouldn't be happening. He was dead—how could anyone grab him and slam him to the ground? Leather Man shouldn't have even been able to touch him in the first place.

66

So why was Sam lying on the gravel?

Senyllia's magic had obviously stopped working. No one was supposed to know about any of this. He was supposed to be able to proposition any female, nail her without her or anyone else knowing, then escape without consequence. It was the only way he could successfully do his work as the Lust Demon's servant.

But something had happened to mess up the works. He had been seen, discovered, and apprehended. Now he was in the process of being mauled by a leather-clad mountain of muscle, gnarly hair, and huge hands.

Just then, he remembered something Senyllia had said, and things began making sense.

"You shall be given back your mortal body before you depart from these chambers. You cannot act as my pawn without a mortal body."

That explained the last couple of minutes—being yanked out of the truck, slammed to the gravel, and the intense pain that followed.

He was dead, but he still had his mortal body. And everyone knew that a mortal body experienced pain.

Sam tried crawling away but was immediately yanked to his feet and slammed against the girl's truck. A solid bony fist pounded his gut. He doubled up and would have fallen down again, but Leather Man kept him mashed tightly against the big vehicle with his free hand.

While doubled up, Sam felt cool air on his fly. He looked down at himself. His pants were still undone, exposing his genitals. He made a feeble effort to pull them up, but Leather Man shoved a hand under his chin, slamming his head against the truck. Sam's cheek smacked against the window. When he opened his eyes, he was pounded once again in the gut. Bright, twinkling stars scurried across his vision. Hot waves of pain shimmered down his back and across his torso. All he could do was watch helplessly as his attacker hauled off a third time.

Leather Man's arm abruptly stopped short. The blonde had rushed over and grabbed his forearm, putting her weight on it. Leather Man yelled a stream of cusswords. He pulled away and tried shaking her off. She bit his hand, driving a loud gasp from his lips. Enraged, he let go of Sam, slapped her with his free hand, and pushed her away.

Sam immediately took off toward the parked vehicles. He slipped between two beat-up muscle cars and made a beeline for the woods.

Heavy footsteps followed not far behind.

Leather Man had apparently shaken free of the girl. He charged after Sam, yelling and cursing. The girl kept up with him, screaming and pounding the brute between the shoulder blades.

Sam disappeared in the trees. If he could widen the distance between them, he might be able to double back to fetch the Camaro. He didn't have time to do much else. Judging by the increased sound of the footsteps behind him, Leather Man was steadily closing the gap.

Sam had apparently underestimated his attacker. The jerk was big, drunk, and somewhat bulky, but could obviously run at a fairly fast clip. The adrenaline pumping through his system had no doubt propelled him. The fact that he had just caught his girlfriend with another man no doubt proved an influencing factor. He was also a little more than mildly upset about his girlfriend biting his arm.

Sam didn't care about the man's motivation. He just wanted to get away. He needed to find a place to hide and hoped Leather Man would eventually give up and return to the bar.

Sam dodged past a cluster of scrub oaks and jumped over a thicket of bushes. He didn't lose a step in his running. The woods were dark, but the moonlight permitted him to see where he was going.

He kept his steady pace, veering around trees and other growth. The footfalls chasing him had lowered in volume, telling him he had gained distance. A wash of relief flowed down his back.

To gauge his progress, Sam suddenly turned around for a glimpse of Leather Man. As a result, he lost his footing, tripped over a deadfall, dropped roughly to the ground, rolled over a rise, and fell down a steep hill.

And kept falling.

And falling.

The ground quickly turned into total darkness.

Falling, falling…

More darkness.

Then, without warning, he landed with a harsh thump on the hot, muddy ground.

The wind was knocked out of him. He lay there, gasping for air. Then, after what seemed an eternity, he sat up and glanced at his surroundings.

The air was hot—much hotter than just a few minutes ago. Foul, too. He wondered if someone was burning something in the bushes not far away.

It smelled almost like...*sulfur*...

Darkness. Burning cinders. A growing sourness filled the air. A sense of dead. Of decay. Of filth.

Shit. He had come back.

About twenty feet away, surrounded by her circle of burning coals, the familiar naked figure sat on her glittering throne, watching him curiously.

Chapter 7

"What is wrong with you, Maggot?"

Long tongues of blue flame gushed thickly from Senyllia's parted lips. "Why are you such a worthless piece of slime?"

Sam backed away from the intense heat. It felt like someone had just opened an oven door just inches from his face.

"Actually, I've been wondering about that same thing myself, but for some reason, I just can't seem to understand—"

"Shut up!"

Angry flames surged toward him, blinding him and turning everything around him into a seething darkness. It took him quite a while to get his vision back. And when he was able to look in her direction, he noticed that her entire form had turned bright red, and the flames still encircled hr.

Senyllia was obviously much angrier than he had ever seen her. Sam realized right then that levity was not exactly the best strategy for him right now

But he couldn't help wondering what he had done to be brought back...

"You *are* paying attention to me, are you not? You had *better* not make me think you are not--"

"I'm paying attention. I'm just trying to figure out why you brought me back."

"I brought you back for a very important reason."

"Which is?"

"You will know that reason as soon as you answer my question."

"Just what was that again?"

She groaned. "I repeat…why are you such a worthless piece of slime?"

He had no idea what to say in his defense. "Is this what you'd call a *trick* question?"

Sparks shot from her mouth like hot spittle with each word she spoke. "You know *not* to trifle with me, Maggot!"

"I honestly didn't know I was."

"You are. Very much so."

"All right. I'm a worthless piece of slime. There. Satisfied?"

"I am *not* satisfied, Maggot! I've already told you what pleases me. And, of course, what does not."

"I know."

She raised a thick red brow. "Really?"

"Of course. Sex. Lots and lots of it. Lust. Lots and lots of that, too. After all, you're the Lust Demon. Lust pleases you."

"It pleases me greatly, Maggot. It is my passion. You knew that before I sent you back to the land of the living. So why are you back here?"

He found her question both odd and suspicious. "Didn't *you* bring me back?"

Her ear-splitting scream tore through the foul darkness. She pounded the stone arms of her throne with her fists. The frothy lust juice covering her sprayed everywhere. Drops splashed the flames surrounding her throne, causing the stone to hiss like angry snakes. The sourness in the air thickened.

He covered his ears and turned away. This babe really had a healthy set of lungs.

"I am *not to be trifled with*, Samuel Hughes!"

"I'm not *trifling* with you—"

"You are!"

He knew better than argue with her, but he had to convince her he was sincere. "I really wish you'd tell me why you think I am..."

She sat back and sighed. The valley between her huge rack deepened. A low-pitched groan escaped her throat. She flicked a thick four-foot-long knot of red hair away from her face. "If you are not trifling with me, then tell me how I am to be satisfied."

"Sex."

"Go on."

"As I just said, lots of it."

"What *kind* of sex?"

He shrugged. "All kinds?"

"Idiot. I told you what I like. You also told me what *you* like. Why have you not already done it?"

"Done what?"

"Stop acting like a classic dunderhead bore." She raised her hand and held it in front of her. Each nail was at least six inches long. "I will shove one of these up your nostril and yank out your brain. I'm hoping I will be able to find *some*thing in there."

"*Please* don't do that..."

73

She shrugged a bare shoulder. "Why shouldn't I? You obviously have great difficulty using it."

"It would…it would really hurt. And leave me with a horrible empty feeling. Besides, it sounds disgusting—"

"*Silence!*"

Sam went silent.

Her eyes simmered. Icy needles shot from them, tingling him. The tips of her breasts pointed straight outward. Her glistening sex dripped onto her seat.

"You have no idea what this is all about, do you?"

"No, sir—*ma'am*. Lady Senyllia."

"You have told me that you enjoy sex. Rough. Forced. Desperate. Hot. Steamy."

"That's what I've been doing."

Her laugh sounded like the angry bark of a large dog. "Samuel Hughes, you are an idiot. A moron. You are also a *clueless* idiot and moron."

"I've been told that before. But could you please be more specific? Sometimes I get confused and…"

"*Silence!*"

Sam sighed.

"You shall listen well, or suffer the consequences. I am not accustomed to repeating myself. This will be the last time I tell you what I expect from you. Do you understand?"

"I guess so…"

"You either understand or you do not!"

He could see himself being tossed like yesterday's trash to another demon, one that wasn't as easy on the eyes as this one. "I totally understand."

"You turned down three females while you were up there. Why did you do that?"

Uh-oh...

She was talking about the hookers he had encountered at the bar. At the time, he thought he wasn't supposed to turn down anyone, but figured he could make up for it. Anyway, how was Senyllia to know?

However, judging by her present demeanor—plus the fact that she had yanked him back down into the bowels of Hell in a heartbeat—he guessed that he was supposed to nail anything who looked at him.

"I am waiting, Samuel Hughes. You had the chance to gratify me using three hookers. Yet you failed to even consider them."

"I don't *like* hookers." He saw no reason to lie.

"You turned down *sex!*" Her expression was one of total disgust. She made it sound like he had run over a puppy.

"I was doing it with that skinny blonde when—"

"You shall *not* turn down *anyone* again! *Ever!*"

"No one?"

"That is what I just said!"

"Even if I find someone ten seconds later?"

"I have not decided to use you because of your discriminating tastes, Samuel Hughes. As I have already stated, I have chosen you because you happen to be nothing more than a dick on two legs."

"That's the *only* reason?"

"What else is there?"

He shrugged. "I thought, maybe you *liked* me--
"

Her shrill laughter shattered the darkness like the screeching of a disoriented banshee. "I am a *demon*, Maggot. Have you *no* knowledge of demons?"

"Just what I've seen in TV shows and horror movies."

"Let me give you a quick lesson. There are just two things you need to know about us. The first one is this: demons don't like *anyone*. And the other, of course, is that demons hate *everyone*."

"Everyone?"

"It is why we are demons. What makes us demons. What keeps us *remaining* demons."

"Makes sense."

"I am glad you are finally able to understand *some*thing."

"So then, I have to nail *every* female I come across?"

"Is there a problem, Samuel Hughes?"

"Not really..."

"By your reaction, I sense a problem. If there is, I can relieve you of your bondage to me and turn you over to one of the other demons. I am sure any one of them will take you. That is another thing about demons, Samuel Hughes. We thoroughly enjoy our toys."

He could only imagine what would happen if he told her he didn't want to do this. But he *should* want to, shouldn't he? He had been a womanizer nearly his entire life. He loved women. Even now. He was dead and he still loved women.

So why was he having a problem with this?

He had to get over this. When he was alive, he could be selective. But he wasn't alive any longer. If he wanted to remain in the mortal world as a man with total power over women, he would have to knuckle down and get with the program.

"I can do this," he told her.

"See that you do." Her breasts jutted out proudly as she straightened on her throne. "This is how my power is fed. What it needs to survive. What I need to remain a powerful demon. When a female collapses in the throes of orgasm, its essence escapes, splashes to the ground, and seeps into the soil. It eventually trickles down here, into my chamber. This makes the coals surrounding my throne sizzle and burn. The hot, gooey juices of lust drip upon them and nourish my power. Lust is my sustenance, Samuel Hughes. The reason for my existence."

He looked straight up but could not see anything beyond the darkness. The mortal world was up there somewhere, but he was unable to catch any glimpse of it. He wondered if he would be able to see an actual shower cascading down if he aimed a powerful spotlight toward the top.

But he knew better than mention it. He didn't want her to turn him into a slug once again for

77

providing humor to the situation. If demons hated mortals, they certainly would not appreciate mortal humor.

"I understand," he said.

"I will send you back up, then."

"You won't be sorry."

"I better not be. If you give me just one more reason to reconsider, I will make things much easier for you to do your job more efficiently. This delay must not happen again."

Damn. What the hell did *that* mean?

"I do not wish to see you again. I wish only to experience and enjoy your accomplishments. I expect to see much of it. Good-bye, Samuel Hughes."

He was still uneasy about what she had said only moments ago. "What did you mean by—"

Blackness. The searing heat quickly dissipated.

***

Sam opened his eyes.

He was lying on the ground in a grove of scrubs just a few yards behind the Quarter Horse statue next to the Western Trail Bar & Grill building.

It was still dark. Most of the vehicles remained parked in the same place as they were when he had first pulled in. The muffled throbbing of the juke caused a heavy pulsing sensation on the ground.

His Camaro hadn't budged from its place. He wondered where Leather Man and Blondie had gone. He also wondered if they had reconciled. Or if one of them had murdered the other.

He decided he didn't care.

Why should he? He was back. That was all that mattered.

He found his keys, straightened, brushed off his trousers, and got behind the wheel.

He was tired but summed it up as the result of his second trip down into the depths of Hell. Nothing to worry about. After some sleep and breakfast, he would be just as good as new.

Tomorrow was Saturday. At least he didn't have to go in to work. He would spend the day doing exactly what Senyllia wanted.

But he couldn't stop wondering what she meant by "making things much easier" for him if she didn't consider his work as useful as she demanded.

Chapter 8

Sam awoke around nine.

He sat up in bed and looked around..

Was he truly home again? In his own apartment?

Back in the land of mortals?

As far as he could tell, this was definitely his apartment. If he had his way, he'd stay here. Hell was damned hot. Foul-smelling. Terrible. Each time he went down, something nasty happened to him. He was more determined than ever to do whatever it took to keep from taking the plunge down there again.

He stepped into the shower and let the steady warm stream beat down on him for twenty minutes to rid himself of any residual almond or sulfur scents still clinging to him. After toweling off, he dressed and made a pot of coffee and a large breakfast of eggs, bacon, toast, and sausage.

As he ate, he thought about his plans for the day.

He immediately settled on a trip to Georgy's Girls Galore in Kissimmee. Although he had gone there half a dozen times before, he had never been able to score with any of the dancers. The babes were sizzling hot, but the bouncers were human tanks and would toss you out onto the sidewalk if you got within two feet of the dancers. Everyone knew that the girls belonged to the club's owners. It was also common knowledge that the babes were off-limits to anyone who didn't drive a Rolls Royce, own a corporation, or personally know the owners.

Each time Sam had gone there, he spent more than a hundred dollars on drinks and lap dances, got back in the Camaro, and drove home half-drunk and hornier than ever.

But that was before Senyllia.

Before he had become one of her servants.

Before he had been given a power that any man on earth would have sold his soul to possess.

A broad grin stretched his cheeks as he thought about the position he was now in. After he had finished his breakfast, he would put this new power to the ultimate test.

***

The huge pink-and-blue two-story Spanish villa, sitting on a five-acre parcel of commercial real estate one mile north of Kissimmee on South Orange Blossom Trail, advertised the best dancers in the area. The club, so the local rumor went, was run by the Mob. "Georgy" was the nickname of Giorgio DeAngelis, a local underground figure well known for buying up prime real estate and handing it over to his sons and nephews, who turned the new venture into a strip club, adult bookstore, or sex novelty shop.

Georgy's was one of the many strip clubs in the area under surveillance by undercover cops. However, its notoriety did much in helping its business. Its enormous parking lot remained filled six nights a week.

At a few minutes past one, Sam parked in an aisle about halfway down from the front entrance. He got out of the Camaro and moved down the center aisle, toward the building, where two human tanks in loose-fitting suits blocked the front door, collecting twenty bucks from everyone wanting to go inside.

Sam's plan was to buy a drink in the main room, then work his way over to one of the lap-dancing areas. He was curious to see if his new power would work on one of the lap dancers. He was also curious to see what would happen if one of the dancers showed an interest in a customer who drove a second-hand Camaro instead of a Rolls.

The club had three separate areas for lap dancing. It was commonly known that only the wealthiest, most important patrons were allowed in the Platinum Room. This enclosed area, located in the rear of the huge building, provided direct access to the dressing rooms and the rear staircase. After her performance, a dancer could escort her elite customer out through the back, up the stairs and into one of the many rooms provided for more private entertainment.

It was a damned terrific deal if you were well-to-do and known in the right circles. Otherwise, you would have to settle for checking out the other two areas, or one of the dozen or so peepshows provided. The bouncers would not let anyone not on the "elite list" anywhere near Platinum.

Sam was determined to gain access. He just didn't know how he could get past the bouncers.

There had to be a way. He figured it would be worth the trouble. The hottest chicks in Central Florida worked that room.

When he was about fifty feet from the front entrance of the building, a gray Lincoln Town Car coaxing down the aisle stopped beside him. The window quietly eased down. The driver, a well-dressed woman about forty-five years old, said, "Young man, I think I took a wrong turn. I'm new to the area. Could you tell me how I can find Lake Buenaventura—"

Then she stopped. Her gaze stayed on him.

Before Sam could react, the woman's eyes had lowered. She slammed the car into park and crawled over the console, until her face cleared the opened window.

Her gaze stopped at his crotch.

Panic stabbed at him. He turned sharply toward the building. *Don't look at her. You're just twenty steps away from the building. Inside, the hottest babes in the city are dancing naked, just waiting for you to show them your new power.*

He wanted to move away. To ignore her. To go back in time, just a few minutes, just as he was getting out of the Camaro. If he could do it, he would run down that aisle and disappear inside the building.

But he knew it was too late.

"Get in, honey."

"No, that's all—"

"I said, *get in!*"

Once again he considered getting away. *Just take off and run down the aisle the rest of the way. Toss your twenty at one of the gorillas at the door, then—*

Senyllia: *"You shall not turn down anyone again!"*

If he rejected this middle-aged bitch, he would find his ass back in Hell quicker than he could blink an eye.

Damn. Damn, damn, damn!

Sighing deeply, he opened the passenger door and got in.

The woman's right hand immediately went to his crotch, covering it. Her left hand continued gripping the steering wheel. She hurried down the aisle, turned left, and pulled into the first vacant spot available.

After she had slammed it into park, her hands attacked his belt, unbuckling it, and opening his jeans.

Sam closed his eyes, sat back, and let her work. He gritted his teeth, tensed his whole body, and waited.

Luckily for him, it didn't take long at all.

***

Fifteen minutes later, Sam, feeling like he had just been mauled, staggered down the aisle of the front lot.

A hundred yards behind him, the Town Car remained parked in its spot. When he left her, the woman remained slouched behind the wheel, gazing stupidly at the windshield. She was probably trying to recall why she was parked in front of a strip club instead of looking for Lake Buenaventura. And why her hair, face, and lips glistened with slobber and sperm.

He cursed himself once again for his stupidity.

He needed to stop mesmerizing females he didn't want to nail. He knew how difficult that would be, but he had to do it. Otherwise, he would end up wasting his time with females he actually didn't care about and wouldn't have time for the hot babes.

He didn't *want* to nail just anything. He had high standards. He had always been attracted to the cream of the crop. And why shouldn't he? Especially now that he was dead and possessed special powers.

But what about Senyllia?

She would know if he turned down sex again.

But how?

How did she find out the first time?

The only way she could have possibly known was if she had some sort of connection with him.

He immediately wondered about those flames she had shot out at him.

Could that be the connection? A spider squirted out her web, cocooning her victims to keep them helpless and immobile. This way, she was able to inject them with her venom so she could devour them later on. Could a demon employ a special kind of fire or flame for this same purpose?

He had originally thought the flames were some sort of technique she used to give him the powers he needed to accomplish his tasks. But since she hadn't given him any explanation whatsoever, he was going to have to figure this out on his own.

She hadn't done anything else out of the ordinary—except for turning him into a slug. But that was just to teach him a lesson. He thought it merely a sort of temper tantrum for a demon. His comeuppance. He hadn't thought for a moment that it served any other purpose.

He realized that if he were being monitored by the Demon of Lust, he would no longer have the luxury to be selective. Like it or not, he was forced to do as she said. Otherwise, he would be brought back to Hell—this time, for good.

He knew he was being silly, that he might be giving her too much credit. There was no possible way Senyllia could constantly monitor him. If she had so many others working for her, how could she monitor them all? How could she monitor anyone while she was talking to him? She wasn't a god; she was a demon. She possessed frightening powers, but how could she possibly know what all her subjects were doing at any given moment?

Despite her demands, he knew he would have to use his powers to his best advantage. This, of course, would have to be done very discreetly. He would have to be particularly careful about where he went and who he encountered. And he would have to be more alert. And infinitely more sensitive to what was going on around him.

His mind made up, he went up the front steps of the club and handed over his twenty to one of the gorillas guarding the front door. The moment the door was pushed open, he slipped inside the dark, air-conditioned area, where the carpeted hall led to the pay phones, restrooms, and lobby leading into the main bar.

The large room swarmed with well-dressed customers bumping elbows with harried waitresses in skirts, halter tops, and high heels. The waitresses were large-breasted, long-haired, and blazing hot. He was careful not to stare at any of them so soon. He wanted to see what was going on in the Platinum Room first. But he could well imagine major complications if his plan went south. If he were forced to settle for a waitress before graduating to a Platinum babe, word would get around very quickly and the human tanks would toss him out and bar him from the club.

Most of the barstools were occupied. Two barmen worked briskly, mixing drinks and setting fresh orders carefully onto round silver trays the waitresses had placed on the counter.

Sam ordered a Manhattan. He only had to wait a few moments before one of the barmen fixed the drink and placed it on the counter in front of him. He dropped a ten-spot on the counter. It was scooped up so quickly, he barely saw the movement.

He finished his drink in one swallow and got right back up. He then joined the slow-moving crowd inching down the softly lit hall, where lap-dancing signs had been posted every twenty feet or so.

A maroon curtain blocked the doorway of the room behind the sign marked *Silver*. A small group of half a dozen guys stopped abruptly, then pushed through the curtain in single file.

The rest of the crowd kept moving.

Sam followed.

Another batch stopped in front of the curtain concealing the second doorway. This one was marked *Gold*. After a few silly remarks, five half-drunk customers tottered past the curtain.

Sam stayed close behind the remaining three guys as they hurried down the hall.

At the end of the hall, a black metal sign marked *Platinum* in white stenciled lettering stood on a stand in front of an archway covered with another maroon curtain. A huge, broad-shouldered guy with a shaved head blocked the curtain, watching them closely. He was about six-five and probably weighed in at around two-eighty. The seams of his jacket were stretched to the limit. He looked like he would tear the jacket to shreds if he bent over or reached up to scratch the top of his head.

When the three guys in front of Sam approached the bouncer, the big man shook his head. His blank expression did not change. "Off-limits" came out flatly. He sounded bored.

The tall, slender man on Sam's right said, "I manage the Kissimmee Savings and--"

"Don't matter. Take a hike."

The short, thickset guy in the middle said, "I've got a friend who knows one of the girls who works in there and says that if I mention her name--"

"You, too."

The tall, heavyset man on the left said, "I have a fleet of limos, and I—"

The bouncer shook his head.

The three men started protesting.

The bouncer produced a cell phone and punched one button. He pocketed the phone seconds later. "There'll be two other guys here in one minute, both my size. Unless you get your butts outa here—"

"All right, all right…"

"This place really sucks."

"Spend a small fortune in here and they treat ya like shit."

Mumbling, they stomped down the hall.

The bouncer grabbed his cell again. "Cancel that last one. Everything's fine." Then he pocketed it and stared curiously at Sam. "What's *your* problem?"

Sam shrugged. "My problem is that I don't *have* a problem."

"Ya will if you don't turn around and join your friends."

"I don't know those guys."

"Don't matter." He pointed down the hall. "Your money's good anywhere but right here."

"I'd like to see what's in here."

"Listen, Slick—"

"Sam."

"You ain't allowed in there, Jack."

"Sam."

"If I were you, buddy, I'd—"

"Sam. And I'm not your buddy."

"That does it." He made another move for his cell.

It was time for an experiment. If Senyllia had given him powers to do her bidding, she might have given him more than he originally thought. If not, then he would know for sure. "Look into my eyes."

The bouncer froze. He held the cell about six inches from his ear. "What?"

"You heard me."

"Why the hell should I—"

"Because I said so."

"Listen, Jack—"

"You really need to improve your short-term memory. My name is *Sam*."

"You're about to get your ass tossed out."

"Cut out the badass cowboy shit and look at me. Just for a second."

"Who the fuck do ya think you're—"

Sam stared right back. *Sleep,* he thought. *Relax. You see nothing right now. You feel nothing. Your entire body is now totally relaxed. No stress. No worries. Life is good...*

The bouncer's tiny light-blue eyes glazed over. His jaw dropped. He began to snore quietly. Drool gathered on his lower lip, gleaming in the overhead lighting. His arm dropped; his hand opened. The cell phone fell quietly to the carpet.

Grinning, Sam picked up the man's phone and put it back in the gorilla's jacket pocket. He slipped away quietly and pushed through the opening in the curtain.

Chapter 9

The huge room was small and dark. Three small spotlights positioned in the ceiling pointed to three different areas. Even in the darkness Sam could tell all four walls were covered with curtains.

A padded chair highlighted the small round stage in each section. A man sat in each chair, his jacket opened, his tie pulled down, his shirt unbuttoned. His arms were pulled behind his back, his wrists handcuffed.

The gorgeous babe moving sensuously in front of each man was no doubt the one responsible for his disheveled appearance. As well as the handcuffs.

Loud, pulsating music flowed into the room, its rapid beat providing the atmosphere with the appropriate mood.

Each dancer wore black mesh stockings and black spiked heels. Each wore her hair long and full, and used it to slap her customer, blindfold, and/or gag him.

No bouncer was needed in this room to supervise the activities. Such protection wasn't necessary. These customers were wealthy, and voluntarily chose the evening's festivities.

The handcuffs also eliminated any possible risk to the dancer.

The working dancer on the far-right side of the room had long black hair, large round tits, and a perfect ass. She looked Asian. With an exaggerated roll of her head, she slapped her customer sharply in the face with her hair, causing him to moan and squirm in the chair. Straddling his chair and bending toward him, she wrapped a thick rope of her hair around the back of his neck and pulled his face forcefully into her chest. Writhing sensuously with the frenzied piped-in beat, she moved in even closer and sat on his lap. She then kissed and tongued him while rubbing his chin with her breasts and squirming in his lap. Sufficiently agitated, he began jerking in the chair. She then reached down between them and fiddled with his trousers.

The honey blonde in the middle spot possessed a set of huge knockers that barely moved as she danced. Squatting over her customer, she pulled her hair back, cupped her boobs in her hands, and rubbed them against the man's face. She held his head in her hands, keeping his face buried while applying the smother technique. He struggled in the chair, his wrists jerking at the handcuffs. The chain clinked loudly against the back of his chair. She released his head and let him catch his breath, then repeated the procedure. While he gasped for breath, she squatted between his spread thighs and went to work with her hands and lips.

The redheaded babe in the third spot straddled her customer. Her hands on her hips, she arched her back and rubbed the man's face with her large tits. He struggled in his chair while she forced him to lick her. Grabbing his hair, she smothered him until he nearly collapsed.

Sam chose the redhead for his first conquest of the afternoon. She appeared the classiest of the three. He liked her hair, her face, and her tits. Her ass was perfect. He couldn't wait to violate every delicious inch of her.

He walked over and stopped a foot or so from the chair. "Sorry to bust up this little shindig, but I've got better ideas about how this ends up."

The man abruptly pulled his face away from the redhead and gawked at him. She straightened sharply, twisting in his direction. Frowning, she looked him over. Confusion covered her fine features. "You're in the wrong room, Mister!"

Sam could not take his eyes off her tits. "Not from this angle, I'm not."

"Get the hell out, asshole." The guy in the chair glared. His wet cheeks had splashed crimson. "We're busy!"

"Really?"

"Any moron could figure *that* one out."

"If you don't mind," Sam said, "I'm borrowing your bodacious buddy for a few minutes."

He struggled to stand, but his pants were halfway down, and his handcuffed wrists made sudden movement difficult. "The fuck you are!"

"Don't blow your wad, dude. I'll return her in an hour or so. She'll probably even be in the same condition."

"Listen, ace. You're in the wrong room and you're messing with the wrong guy. And this is definitely the wrong fucking time for bullshit!"

"When will the right fucking time be?"

"You're an asshole. Get out."

"I've been told that a few times before. Both the asshole part and the get out part."

"Listen good, dirtbag. You're about to get your ticket punched as well."

"Not from you, obviously."

His eyes grew. "Do you happen to know who I am?"

Sam shrugged. "Don't *you* know who you are?"

"Listen, smartass. I happen to be--"

"Yeah, I know who you are. You're the guy sitting there wearing a pair of handcuffs. Your pants are down, you're all exposed and just as helpless as a newborn, and you're still trying to sound like a badass. Unless you're Harry Houdini and can get out of those cuffs in two seconds, you're not exactly much of a threat to me right now."

"I don't have to do *anything*, you idiot. All I have to do is call Flip in here. Then I can just sit here—still cuffed, by the way—and watch him fold you into neat little bite-sized pieces before he takes you out to the dumpster. I don't know how the hell you got past him, but--"

"He was taking a nap when I came in."

"Bullshit. Flip doesn't nap while he's working."

"Maybe he overdid it at the gym, or the all-you-can-eat burger fest they're having down the street."

"Cut the bullshit. All I have to do is yell, and he'll be in here before you can figure out just how stupid you really are. He'll pick your sorry ass up and toss it right out the—"

95

Sam focused. The man's eyes glazed over.

The redhead looked worried. "Lou?" She glanced at Sam, then at her customer. "What the *hell*..." She twisted around and glared at Sam. "W-What did you *do* to him?"

Sam gave the redhead the same stare. Her eyes glazed over as well. A moment later, her eyes lowered, and she reached for his crotch.

***

The redhead opened her eyes and stared at her surroundings.

Her gaze lingered on the bed immediately to her left. Then she lowered her head and studied the carpet.

Sam could tell she was trying to remember. She knew she was on her knees but couldn't recall coming here or even lowering herself into this position. When she straightened, her hair had fallen over her face. She brought up both hands and pushed the heavy red curtain over her shoulders. Then stared at his genitals.

She was still fighting hard to remember.

She stared at him as if seeing him for the first time. Her makeup was all blotched and runny. Drops of his semen stained her lips, chin, and both tits. She brought up a hand, wiped her chin, and stared at her palm. Then at him. She still obviously couldn't put it all together.

"What...did you *do*?" she asked in an unsteady whisper. "How'd I...get *here*?"

"You led me out through the back and brought me upstairs." Sam went over to the table opposite

96

the bed, where various S&M instruments sat in neat rows. It was time to get this show on the road. He was far from finished with this babe. He wanted to drench Senyllia's lust chamber with fresh orgasmic juices.

"By why...why am I *here*? With *you*?" She pushed more hair away from her face. "I'm supposed to be working till six. That means I'm scheduled to be with that guy—Lou—the guy I was just with."

"What's wrong with *me?*"

"I don't even *know* you, baby. I don't even remember how I got *up* here..."

"I told you. You brought me up."

"Wh-What did you *do?* I mean, I don't remember *anything*! It's like, like I just...just...woke *up*..." She gently touched her wet cheeks and chin. "Did I just...suck you off?"

"You could say that."

"Something's totally *wrong*."

He grinned. "I think everything's just fine."

She rubbed her temples and, swaying a little, got to her feet. She was forced to lean on the mattress to prevent herself from stumbling. Then she discovered more wet spots on her neck and collarbone. She wiped her skin, stared stupidly at the result, then wiped her palm on the bed sheet. She turned to him and frowned. "I was downstairs with Lou. He had me for two hours." She glanced at the small digital clock on the night table. "I should still be down there."

"I convinced you to come upstairs with me."

97

"But I'm not allowed to *do* that! If Donnie finds out--"

"I won't tell if you won't."

"Listen, Mister--"

"Sam."

"Listen. Sam? Donnie's sure to find out. Was Lou still there when we left?"

"Sure was."

Her eyes grew. "What...was he doing?"

"Not much."

"Whaddya mean?"

Sam shrugged. "You can't do too much at all with your pants down and you're handcuffed to a chair."

She sighed and shook her head. "Shit, shit, shit! This is just *awful!*"

"He had a really stupid expression on his face, too. He looked totally bummed out."

She covered her mouth with her palm. "You didn't...you didn't knock him *out*, did you?"

"Of course not. I'm not a *thug*, you know."

"Then how did you...how *could* you...how were you able to...to--"

"I put a spell on him."

"A *what?*"

"A spell."

Her eyes grew, filling the sockets. "You mean...you're some sort of...*witch*?"

"I wouldn't put it quite *that* way. Let's just say I have a few talents most people don't know too much about."

She stared at him uneasily. He could tell she was afraid. Her eyes were enormous. "How'd you...I mean, what'd you do...to convince him...to let you...take me away?"

"I suggested he take a nap. He decided that might not be a bad thing to do. It turned out that he really needed one." Sam shrugged. "What you were doing takes a lot out of a guy."

She began pacing. "This isn't good. I'm toast. Really and truly. Donnie doesn't fuck around. I won't be able to work anymore. He'll mess me up, make sure I never work anywhere around here ever again." She stopped and glared at him. "Mister, you really fucked me forever when you did whatever you did to get me to bring you up here."

"Listen. Since we're already here, and since you've just made the suggestion, we might as well--"

"I've got to get out. I mean it." She grabbed her robe from the armchair. "I've got to get back to my dressing room. I really need to get out of this room. My clothes—"

"You won't need them."

She shrugged into her robe. "Mister, I've got to explain to Donnie what happened!"

"But you really *don't* know what happened."

"Then that's what I've got to tell him!"

"Do me a large favor."

"What's that?"

"Get out of that irritating robe and lie down on the bed."

She gasped. "You just don't understand!"

99

"Sure I do. You're the one who doesn't."

"I'm scared, Mister. Really and truly scared! Donnie, he—you've got to understand. Donnie's not like anyone else. He's—"

"No need to be scared, baby. Just squirm out of that robe and we'll—"

"These guys don't mess around. They're mean. They carry things around with them."

"Like what?"

"Brass knuckles. Switchblades. Box-cutters. One of them has this roll of quarters he uses when a girl—" She shivered. "Like I said, they *don't mess around!*"

"Neither do I."

"Ever hear of Georgy DeAngelis?" Her voice quickly trailed down to a whisper.

"What's *he* have to do with all this?"

"He *owns* this place!"

"Hell, everyone knows that."

She stared at him as though she could not believe what he just said. "He's someone you *really* don't want to mess around with, Mister."

"Sam."

"Mister...Sam."

"You're the only one I want to mess around with, baby."

"But you don't--"

"Just get naked and lie down. We'll have a little fun, then you can leave and go back downstairs."

She shook her head. "That's not how it works, Mister!"

100

"Sam. How's it work?"

"The guy I was doing down there?"

"What about him?"

"He owns things. Lots and lots of things. Hotels. A casino. He's a rich, important guy. He gave me five thousand for two hours and you went and fucked it all up!"

As she rambled, Sam checked the items on the table. Loops of clothesline. A thick roll of duct tape. An assortment of silver clamps. Handcuffs. Nipple rings. Ball gags. A submission helmet with convenient snaps for a gag and blindfold attachment.

Sam grinned. He was going to have some genuine fun with this babe. "Looks like you've got some toys that will come in handy."

She gawked at the toys arranged on the table and cringed when she saw the expression on his face. "That stuff…it's only for certain clients, baby. Like I said, I don't even *know* you! You could be a cop! Besides, I need to go back downstairs and square this with Lou." She groaned. "Somehow…"

"Don't worry, I'll let you square it."

She blinked, studying his expression. She apparently believed him. "Good. Great." She sighed tiredly. "I really and truly appreciate it. I just hope I can convince him…" She fastened the sash around her robe and hurried to the door.

He stepped in front of her. "After you do one thing for me."

She shook her head. "Listen, honey. I'm scared. Really and truly scared. Like I said, these guys don't mess around. I'll end up all beat up and scarred, and I won't be able to--"

"Just get out of that robe, lie down on the bed, and we'll—"

"Even if you were a regular customer, I'm not supposed to do that. *I'm* supposed to be the one that does the tying up."

"Never been tied up before?"

She shrugged loosely. "A couple of times." She watched his expression and shrugged. "All right, a lot—okay? In my apartment, mostly. My boyfriend, he likes to do it to me, once in a while. When he says I've been bad and need to be taught some manners. Listen. The boss wants us to do what he says, and—"

Sam focused.

Her eyes glazed over. Sam coaxed her over to the bed and patted the mattress. "Lie down and spread your arms and legs."

She moved zombie-like, obeying him without a word. In seconds she lay completely still, her arms and legs spread wide. Her eyes remained glazed, focused on the ceiling as he fastened her wrists and ankles to the four posts of the bed with clothesline, pulled the submission helmet over her head and carefully applied metal clamps to her nipples and the wet lips of her sex. He then fitted her mouth with a ring gag and secured it into position using the snaps on the submission helmet.

The gag had obviously been designed by an expert. It accommodated him perfectly.

For the next half-hour, Sam had the time of his life.

Chapter 10

Dominic Scarpe, known by his friends and business associates as Donnie Shoes, had been running Georgy's Girls Galore since the place opened five years earlier. Donnie had been running strip clubs the last twenty years and was good at what he did. He knew how to find the right girls, how to handle them, and how to feature them to make the place successful.

Before Georgy's, Donnie made a successful living managing several places in the Miami Beach area for a couple of the local bosses. Donnie had been living in Miami since graduating high school. He liked the weather, the babes, and the atmosphere. But when Georgy the Boss requested his presence in the Central Florida area, Donnie jumped at the chance. Georgy was a great guy to work for. He was fair and generous. And if you made money for the club and kept the cops at arm's length, he left you alone and gave you total reign.

Donnie had never regretted his decision to move to Central Florida. He owned a beautiful palatial estate in Sable Point with its own pool and tennis court. He was also the proud owner of two muscle cars. He had the world by the balls and could easily retire in less than five years with quite an impressive nest egg to enjoy.

Everything had been running smoothly since the place opened. As with all clubs that dealt with booze and gorgeous babes, there were a few minor annoyances. But it was no big thing. Every place on earth had had to put up with occasional bullshit. Sometimes customers had too much to drink and decided to send caution to the wind by groping the waitresses and dancers. Sometimes the wrong folks snooped around to see where the dressing rooms were and had to be redirected. A wise club owner always knew to hire the biggest and most capable bouncers. When you have more than a dozen big boys walking around to keep things quiet, everything turns out fine. And at the end of the day, the kitty always goes to bed fat and happy.

However, as with all aspects in life, things tend to change without warning. Just a few minutes ago, Donnie's office phone rang with Georgy the Boss on the other end of the line, reaming him a new asshole.

"Fucking bozo comes into the place, somehow gets past the bouncer, takes Wendy right out of Platinum, follows her upstairs, and has a big-time ball with her. And where the fuck is her client? This is *Lou Brannon* we're talkin' about, for God's sakes! *Lou Brannon*, Dominic! Why, the guy's left sitting cuffed in his chair, his fucking pants pulled down, his dick hanging out. I want to know how this bozo got in. And how he got past the bouncer. And who the hell the fucking bouncer is. And how Mr. Bozo conned Wendy upstairs. This sort of bullshit doesn't happen in my club, Dominic. I want this taken care of and I want it taken care of *now!*"

105

Donnie knew full well that he was in seriously deep shit. Georgy called him Dominic only when he was really pissed.

But Donnie couldn't blame Georgy for being on the rag. There was no reason in hell why one of their most popular Platinum dancers would up and leave a paying client right in the middle of one of her spots, and without even bothering to take off the damned cuffs.

What the hell was going on here? Flip was one of their best bouncers. The jerk was an animal. Hell, he could bench press a quarter of a ton on one of those weird machines at Gold's Gym. The big boy was gung-ho about his health, too—no booze, drugs, or even fatty foods. Pumped iron six days a week, then drove to the Steakhouse and devoured a two-pound medium-rare Porterhouse before coming to work. Flip could easily snatch up a normal-sized guy, cart the idiot's sorry ass outside, and toss him out in the street.

Flip was a good worker, too. He never bitched about anything and had no reason to. He had a good job that paid for his room, muscle car, all the steak he could eat, and a lifetime membership at Gold's.

So…what the hell was the big moose doing while this bozo walks right in, pulls Wendy off Brannon, and carts her fine ass upstairs?

"Who was watching Platinum?" Georgy asked Donnie.

"That was Flip, Mister D." Donnie hated ratting on his men, but this was Georgy, and you just didn't lie to the big man.

106

"Which one is he?"

"Big, strong, stupid-lookin'."

Georgy groaned loudly. "C'mon now, dammit. Be more specific!"

"Shaved head--"

Another groan. "*Specifics*, goddammit!"

"He's the one, tossed out that Magic asshole a few weeks ago, the one actin' like he owned the place. Fucker was pushin' around everyone, feelin' up the waitresses, talkin' about his big dick, his latest multi-million-dollar contract with the Chinese—"

"Huge black fucker? Too full of himself to tip his waitress?"

"That was him."

"He's a big boy. Strong as an ox, and I've heard he loves his job. So then, what the fuck happened?"

"I intend to find out, Mister D."

"See that you do. This leaks out, I'm gonna have to do some serious head-chopping. I can't afford to let my associates think they can spend five K in my place while some dickhead crawls in off the street and walks off with his prime source of entertainment. *Capisc*?"

"Yes, sir."

"I want you to smooth this over with Brannon as well."

Donnie had no idea how he could do that. Rich guys like Brannon were all alike, toting around that huge ego thing that said they were the best thing in the world since the fucking cell phone. But when something out of the ordinary happened, they went looking for blood like hungry vampires. Smoothing this out would be a bitch and a half, but Donnie knew better than mention this to the Boss. Especially when the Boss sounded like he wanted to chew on a giant box of carpet tacks.

"Yes, sir..."

"Do whatever it takes to make him happy. I don't give a fuck if you have to give him Alicia and Bobby at the same time for free. Just make the man happy. And make damned sure he wants to come back!"

"Yes, sir."

"Lou Brannon spends two hundred K in my places every year!"

"I totally understand—"

"If we lose that account, you lose your job. Maybe even your fucking head." *Click.*

Donnie put down the phone, opened his desk drawer and pulled out a small pint bottle of Wild Turkey. He poured two inches into a glass and sucked it down. Then he took a deep breath and poured another two inches. He put the bottle back, picked up the phone, and punched the appropriate number. When he heard Flip's voice, Donnie said, "What the hell's happenin' in my club?"

"I-I don't know, sir!"

The idiot sure as hell sounded scared. And he really should be.

"What the fuck do you *mean*, you don't know? You were stationed at Platinum. You were guarding it because that happens to be your job. An idiot walks right past you, waltzes into Platinum, grabs Wendy, and takes her upstairs. There was only one way into that room, and it was past you. You know that, right?"

"Yes, sir."

"How'd that crazy idiot get past you?"

"I wish I knew, sir. I was talkin' to him. I told him to go back to the other rooms. Then I closed my eyes, and he was gone."

Donnie stiffened. Was he hearing things? Could this really be happening? "You...fell *asleep*?"

"N-No, sir—"

"You just said you closed your eyes!"

"I-I d-didn't fall asleep—"

"Then why'd you close your eyes?"

"I *blinked*, sir..."

"You what?"

"I blinked."

"You're sayin' you *blinked*?"

"Y-Yes, sir..."

"Then what happened?"

"He...he was gone."

This was getting more and more ridiculous by the second. "He *disappeared*? Is *that* what you're trying to say?"

"I guess I am, sir..."

"You blinked, and he disappeared?"

"Y-Yes, sir—"

"And when you opened your eyes, he was gone?"

"Y-Yes, sir..."

Original. Real original. This sounded pretty much like the latest version of "the dog ate my homework." Punks these days just didn't have the sense—or the imagination—the Almighty gave a chipmunk. When Donnie was finished with this moron, he wouldn't be able to find a job guarding a public shitter.

But there were more important issues to address.

"We'll talk about this later. There are things that need to be done, and you're gonna do them. Understand?"

"Yes, sir."

"Where are you now?"

"I'm out in back."

"What are you doin' *there*?"

"Just looking around…"

Donnie hated when these young punks were unable to show sufficient brain activity. It had to be the steroids; nothing else made any sense. He sighed tiredly. "You're *supposed* to be looking for the dickhead that took Wendy upstairs. Couldn't you figure that one out on your own?"

"He w-wasn't up there, sir. That's why I'm out here, looking around."

"Did you find Wendy?"

"Yes, sir."

"What was *she* doin'?"

A pause. "Nothin'."

This idiot was beginning to grate on Donnie's nerves. If Georgy intended to do some head-chopping, Donnie decided to do a little trimming himself. And he'd sure as hell get rid of Flip if the moron didn't start making sense soon.

"You're really pissin' me off, dammit. Tell me in plain English exactly what Wendy was doin' when you went upstairs and broke into the room."

"I didn't break in, sir."

"Why not?"

"The door was open."

Donnie took a deep breath. "All right, you didn't break in, you just walked in—could I possibly be right?"

"Yes, sir…"

"What was Wendy doin' when you went in there?"

"Nothin'."

"*Nothin'*? At *all*?"

"She…couldn't."

The back of Donnie's neck instantly grew hot. "Why the hell not? Is she…is she okay? Did that dirtbag--"

"She's okay, sir."

"Then what the fuck are you tryin' to say?"

"She was tied to the bed."

"You mean that asshole…that son of a bitch *raped* one of my girls?"

"I…d-don't know, Mr. Shoes."

"What the fuck do you *mean,* you don't know? What did Wendy say?"

"Nothin'."

"Why not? You just said she's okay. If she's actually okay, why didn't she—"

111

"No marks on her. Just that tatt she's got on her ankle and that other one, the one that looks like a horse, it's right near her—"

"Now why would I care about a fuckin' *tattoo*? I'm only interested in what this dirtbag *did* to her. Get it?"

"Yes, sir."

Donnie sucked down more Wild Turkey. At this rate, he was gonna need another bottle shortly. "Then why the fuck wasn't she talkin'?"

"She had a gag…in her mouth, sir."

He was beginning to wonder if these muscle heads actually had anything in their heads but solid meat. "All right, now. Listen to me. I'll talk slow. Did…you… untie…her?"

"No, sir. One of the other dancers--"

"All right. You didn't untie her. Whoever untied her and took the gag out of her mouth is unimportant. What did Wendy say when the gag was taken out?"

"That's just it. She seemed like she was in a daze. She doesn't *know* what happened, or why she was tied to the bed. She seemed to be lookin' around. It was like she was confused."

This was seriously strange. "She might've been drugged, then."

"I don't know, sir. I was gonna ask what happened, but Alicia ran in right then and said Nicole was missing."

Donnie cringed. This was turning into a fucking nightmare. He took a breath to collect himself. After that last visit to the doctor, he was ordered to

112

keep the blood pressure under control or take the big one, like the old man did just ten years earlier. He had no intention of going out so soon. He was *forty-five*, for God's sake. That was too fucking young to kick the bucket—especially when you had a huge nest egg waiting for you in five short years.

He closed his eyes and thought about that aquarium Beth had brought home last month to give the living room a little class and atmosphere. It worked, too. After a long day, he looked forward to driving home, dumping his butt in the La-Z-Boy, and spending the next half-hour watching those expensive tropical fish swim around constantly, eat, and shit. That was all it took for a great calm-down. Everything that had happened earlier just faded away.

Just thinking about those fish worked wonders. Or maybe it was the Wild Stuff kicking in. Whatever it was didn't matter—just as long as *some*thing worked.

"What the fuck do you mean, *missing*?"

"I went downstairs, and Mae Ling was the only one left in Platinum."

"Flip?"

"Yes, sir?"

"You know what you have to do, right?"

"Find that bozo, sir?"

"That would be a good start. Make sure someone's watching the traffic leaving the front lot."

"You really think he's still on property, sir?"

"I could be wrong, but a jerk with enough *cojones* to do what he's been doin' might just want to stick around so he can keep doin' it."

"I'm on it."

"Take two of the other guys with you."

"Yes, sir."

"I also want you to find Nicole."

"Yes, sir."

"Once you find them, I want both of them in my office as quickly as possible."

"Where do you want the bozo, sir?"

"Take him out to the warehouse and stay with him. After the babes tell me what happened, I'll drop by and spend a little time with this asshole, who obviously doesn't seem to care if he lives or dies."

Chapter 11

His pants pulled down to his ankles, Sam relaxed in the comfortable reclining seat of the stretch limo parked in the rear lot of the club. His eyes were closed. A huge grin covered his face as the big-titted blonde from the Platinum Room knelt between his legs.

After she had completed her task, he sat there a few moments, his heart racing.

She remained kneeling before him, her bathrobe opened. Her big blue eyes stared directly at him. Her hair was a matted mess. Her cheeks and chin, as well as the valley between her jugs, shimmered with long trails of his discharge.

"That was great, baby. And very appreciated."

She didn't reply.

"Senyllia will be pleased."

Her blank eyes revealed nothing.

He pulled up his pants and climbed out of the limo, then slipped through the open carport, where a sparkling Ferrari and a vintage Maserati sat in pristine condition.

He crossed the gravel aisle leading to the front of the building and hurried down the sandy road, where the Camaro was parked.

That was definitely enough activity for one afternoon. First, the middle-aged tourist who pleasured him on his way inside the club. Then, the ravaging two of Georgy's hottest babes.

Senyllia was probably grinning stupidly from her throne.

Although he was almost certain exhaustion should have already overwhelmed him, fresh energy flowed from him. He was shocked when he realized he was ready to go all over again.

That stamina thing Senyllia had promised, no doubt.

Why question things when they seemed to be working so well?

Whatever was happening, the cold fact remained. He had to get out of here and find other girls before the club's human tanks caught up to him. They were no doubt seriously pissed that he had taken two of their best girls out of the Platinum Room during peak hours. Because of Sam, they could be fired or severely chastised by their boss. Everyone working there would want his hide.

Best get out while he still could.

Disney Village could be a great prospect for his next excursion. There were always sweet young babes wandering around outside the hotels, looking for all sorts of ways to get into trouble. He could hit on a couple of hot tourists, or maybe even a—

"Hey! You! Hold it!" barked a low-pitched voice behind him.

Sam turned.

Two bouncers rushed toward him. The one closest to Sam held a small automatic pistol. Its snub nose was pointed directly at Sam's face.

Sam wondered what a bullet would do to a dead man. He guessed that it would probably just cause a little pain and aggravation, similar to his encounter with Leather Man's fists. Sam thought that would be a genuine laugh. He would thoroughly enjoy watching everyone's reaction when they hauled him to the Emergency Ward on a gurney, dropping a serious load the moment he jumped up and ran out of the hospital as soon as they pulled the bullet out of his head.

"Problem?" he asked his two new companions.

The two men snickered. The one holding the gun said, "For you, Mister."

"Really?"

"Really. In fact, this is probably gonna be the worst day of your life."

"I wouldn't think so. I just had a terrific time with two of your best girls."

Both glared. The first one said, "Yeah. We know. And it's gonna cost ya."

"Whatever the price, it was worth it. You really ought to give those lovely ladies a raise. They definitely know how to rock a dude's world."

The bouncers turned to one another and laughed loudly.

"Something funny?" Sam asked.

"Yeah," the gunman said. "You thinking you could pull one off on Donnie Shoes."

"Who?"

The bouncers exchanged confused looks. The other one said, "Don't tell me you never heard of Donnie Shoes..."

"I never heard of Donnie Shoes."

"He runs this club."

"I thought Big Georgy—"

"Big Georgy *owns* the club. Donnie Shoes *runs* things."

"Ah. I see. A kind of hierarchy."

Both men looked confused.

"A chain of command, in layman's terms."

The gunman shrugged. "The only thing you need to know is, Donnie's the one who's gonna put your lights out."

Sam shrugged. "You're telling me he's the electrician, right?"

The bouncers both stared. Sam guessed they were trying to figure out why he wasn't scared. He should be shaking in his boots. Or sweating. Possibly maybe even pissing his pants.

They obviously hadn't spent much time talking to a dead man before.

***

Nervously gripping their bathrobes, Wendy and Nicole shuffled unsteadily into Donnie Shoes' office. Flip, looking both embarrassed and angry, followed them in.

"Close the door," Donnie said.

Flip closed the door behind them and went over to stand near the window.

The girls looked as if they had just been run over by a truck. Their makeup was smudged, their hair a mess. They moved stiffly, taking short steps.

Donnie tried reading their expressions. They appeared confused and scared as they huddled close beside one another, their white-knuckled fists clutching their robes. He had never seen them act this way before.

Donnie instinctively knew when people were pulling something. This gift came in handy when you dealt with all sorts of people. In his view, it was damned obvious that these girls weren't pulling anything. Neither was Flip, judging from his troubled expression.

What made all this even more baffling was that all three had always been good employees.

"Start talking," he told the girls.

Neither spoke. Both continued shivering.

"You two cold?"

They both shook their heads.

"Then start talking."

Silence.

Donnie sat back and sighed. He decided that a softer approach might work better. Donnie wasn't exactly the poster boy for "softer approach," but figured he might be able to get it together in this situation. He had nothing to lose—especially since Georgy was on the warpath and demanded answers.

"You left Lou Brannon," he told Wendy in a much softer voice. "You left him exposed and cuffed to the chair. Mind telling me what happened?"

"I don't *know*, Donnie!"

"What the hell do ya *mean*, you don't know?" *Easy, easy...* He took a deep breath and let it back out slowly, as the doc had ordered. "You left one of our best clients with a bozo none of us ever saw before. You left Platinum, took Mr. Bozo upstairs,

119

and let him tie you down. Did he even *pay* you for that?"

She shook her head.

Donnie just sat there, doing his best not to explode. This was totally un-fucking believable. A high-class babe like Wendy walking out on what would surely have turned out to be two or three grand? Then letting herself be tied down, raped by some bozo, and letting him leave without getting paid?

What the hell was going on?

He took a few more deep breaths, closed his eyes, and tried calming himself. *Mellow. Remember what you're supposed to do when the stress tries getting hold of you. Take in the good stuff, let out the bad. Don't let that ticker go bonkers on you. Think of retirement...and all the terrific things you're gonna do when you get the hell out of this racket...*

He took another deep breath and opened his eyes. Then he looked directly at Wendy and said, "Don't wanna tell me why you let him do that?"

She shrugged.

"He pull a gun on you? A knife?"

"I...don't *think* so..."

"You don't *think* so?"

Wendy shook her head.

"That would be somethin' you'd know, wouldn't it? You'd see a knife or gun, wouldn't ya? Especially if it was pointed directly atcha?"

No response.

120

He decided he was being a little rough, so he decided to ease off on Wendy. He took another breath and turned to Nicole. "What about you?"

She shrugged. "All I remember is waking up in one of the stretches, Donnie."

Mellow…and breathe… "You don't remember how the hell you *got* there?"

"No, sir."

This was getting even more ridiculous by the moment. "Talk to me, Flip. How the hell did this idiot get past *you*? And don't give me that fuckin' "he disappeared" shit again."

"Wish I knew, sir."

Donnie poured more of the Wild Stuff into his glass and downed it in one swallow. This was getting *way* the hell out of hand. If he didn't know better, he'd swear everyone had been put in some weird trance, like in one of those stupid horror flicks.

How the hell could someone put Flip under, then con two girls out of their Platinum spots—right in the middle of their routine?

He turned back to Wendy and hoped she had recovered enough during the last few minutes and would start using her brain. "Girl, are you trying to tell me that you left one of our best customers, took some strange asshole upstairs, then let him tie you down so he could do whatever he wanted? He did it for *free*? And he didn't even have a gun or knife?"

"That's what they say happened, Donnie," she said softly.

"She was wearing a sub helmet when we found her, boss," Flip said.

Wendy reddened and lowered her head. Flip's explanation had obviously embarrassed her.

Donnie glared. Some people just didn't know when to keep their mouth shut. "And this explains the situation how?"

Flip shrugged and turned around to look out the window.

"What were *you* wearing?" Donnie asked Nicole.

She shrugged and looked down at herself. "My bathrobe."

"You went outside in your *bathrobe*? With a total *stranger*?"

She nodded.

"And they found you in the back seat? Staring off into space? With your robe all opened?"

"I *guess* so..."

His cell rang. He picked it up.

It was Tommy. "Good news, boss. We got 'im."

"Who?"

"The asshole that did Nicole and Wendy."

It was about damned time. At least *something* had finally happened the way it was supposed to.

"Where do you have him?"

"We're in the warehouse with him."

He jumped up from his seat. "I'll be right down."

"We'll keep him here, boss."

"You'd better, dammit. If I get down there and find you all standin' around with your dicks in your hands, tellin' me you have no idea what happened, you'd better pray I didn't bring along enough bullets with me!"

Chapter 12

Three huge guys in ill-fitting suits led Sam into the big warehouse behind the club. As soon as everyone was inside, the last guy slammed the door shut and stood directly in front of it.

The afternoon sunlight came in through a small, slatted window, providing thick bars of haze that lit up a rectangular portion of the concrete floor in the center of the large open area.

Sam immediately checked out his new surroundings. Crates and boxes filled one corner of the room. Three small offices ran along the opposite wall. Two large vehicles, both covered with canvas tarps, sat just a few feet from the wide roll-up double door.

The big guy holding the gun told him to stay put.

"For how long?" he asked.

The man glanced at his friends and shook his head. He turned back to Sam and shrugged. "Until someone tells you *not* to stay put, smartass."

"What'll happen if I move?"

"You'll be shot right here on the spot."

"By you?"

"Does it matter?"

"Just curious."

"We all have guns, dickhead."

"All three of you?"

The men nodded grimly.

"And all three of you are good shots, too?"

"Just try somethin' and we'll show ya."

Sam grinned. "Sounds dangerous and menacing."

"You sure are actin' stupid for someone who ain't gonna be here much longer," one of them said.

Sam wanted to tell them he was going to be here much longer than any of them could possibly know. He decided not to tell them anything. It would make them curious. When people were curious, they tended to ask all sorts of irritating questions.

Sam was more interested in what they were going to do next. If any of those mobster movies he had seen as a kid served as a guide, they would probably call their boss and have him come here. The boss would threaten Sam with torture and a horrible death, then ask him all sorts of stupid questions. Sam would tell them anything they wanted to know, but no one would believe him. And he couldn't blame them one bit.

The one who had closed the door produced a cell phone and whispered into it. He pocketed it, then came over to where Sam stood between the other two. "Our boss is on his way," he said. "Better say your prayers."

Sam wanted to laugh. Yep, these guys were right out of an old gangster flick. "Your boss...is he that boot guy you mentioned?"

The men stiffened. The one holding the gun said, "His *name*, asshole, is Donnie *Shoes*. *Mister* Shoes to you."

They all looked so *serious*. Apparently this Donnie Shoes was like a god to them. Sam had the feeling that they all wanted to get down on their knees and pray to the god of shoes. It was getting increasingly difficult to keep from laughing.

"Donnie Shoes," he said, shrugging. "Shoes." He shook his head. "Sorry, but I can't help thinking his daddy had helluva sense of humor."

"Listen, you stupid son of a—"

The door banged open.

A dark-haired man around fifty years old marched in, followed by the human tank Sam had confronted outside the Platinum Room.

About five-eight and probably more than two hundred pounds, the first man looked like a character from the *Sopranos*. He wore an expensive tailored three-piece brown suit, a gold tie, and a carnation in the lapel of his jacket. His shoes were patent-leather and probably imported.

Nice, but nothing worth writing home about. Sam expected to see spats, a diamond stud, or something else that would make it more special. Initials, maybe? But there was nothing.

The man stopped about five feet from Sam. He noticed Sam staring at the floor at his feet and gestured to one of the four men. "What the fuck's he looking at?"

"Dunno, boss."

He turned to the guy who had followed him in. "Flip? *You* know what he's looking at?"

"No, sir. Ask him."

"Huh?"

126

Flip shrugged. "He might tell ya, boss."

Their boss considered that for a few moments. Then: "What the fuck you lookin' at, bozo?"

"The name's Sam. I'm looking at your shoes."

The man lowered his head, displaying a pronounced bald spot at the crown. "What the fuck's wrong with my shoes?"

Sam shrugged. "Just trying to figure out why everyone calls you Donnie Shoes. I guess I expected something really special, high-priced, tasteful, and—"

"These puppies go for *two grand a pair*, bozo," the man said in a loud voice. "They're hand-made just for me and shipped over here from Palermo, Italy."

Sam had obviously hit a nerve.

"Yeah, they look pricey. But..." He shrugged.

"But *what*, bozo?"

Sam was quickly growing tired of *bozo*. It was slightly better than Senyllia's *maggot*, but it still bugged him. "My name is Sam. Sam Hughes. I just figured they'd be really top-rate or something." He grinned. "Maybe spats… A racing stripe might be a nice touch."

"You're really a stupid asshole, aren'tcha, bozo?"

This dude obviously had a short memory. "To repeat, my name's *Sam*. And why would you think I'm stupid?"

"I'm about to stop your clock, and here you are, insultin' my shoes."

"I'm not insulting your shoes. They look all right…that is, if you like that kind of thing. A little ostentatious for my taste, though—"

"*What*?"

"Ostentatious. It means rich and showy."

The dude turned red in the face. "I *know* what the fuck it means!"

"Then why'd you look so clueless when I said it?"

The man's eyes blazed. Sam could tell Donnie Shoes wanted to do something violent. It took him a little while to regain his composure. He took a few deep breaths while sizing up Sam. "Flip," he said between clenched teeth, "you stay here. You other three get out. I'm about to do somethin' nasty and I want as few witnesses around as possible when that happens."

"Boss?" The one holding the gun shrugged. "You *sure* about this?" he asked softly.

"Yeah." Donnie Shoes remained glaring at Sam. "I'm fuckin' sure about this. You and your two buddies get your asses out. *Now*!"

"Right now?"

"You deaf or somethin'?" Donnie Shoes shot a quick glare at the man. "Yeah. Right now. This second, dammit! This fucker's pissin' me off and I want to spend some quality time with him before I send him to his Maker."

The three bouncers quickly slipped through the door and slammed it shut behind them.

"Senyllia," Sam said.

Donnie Shoes scowled. "What?"

"Her name is Senyllia."

"*Whose* name, smartass?"

"My Maker."

Donnie Shoes scowled at Sam for long moments before he spoke. He appeared to be trying to read Sam's mind. "What're you talkin' about, dirtbag?"

"Sam. Call me Sam. My Maker is a chick."

Flip moved closer to Donnie Shoes. He didn't take his eyes off Sam. "This boy's crazy, boss. I mean a genuine loony bird."

"Sounds like it, don't it? Talkin' about a *chick* Maker?" Donnie Shoes squinted at Sam. "You're not one of those religious nuts, are ya, asshole?"

"You really have a lot of different names for me. But as I keep trying to tell you, my name's Sam. And no, I'm not religious."

"What the hell's all this shit about some chick you say is named Senile--"

"Senyllia. Her name's Senyllia."

"And just what the fuck does this…this Senyllia chick…have to do with any of this?"

"As I just said, she's my Maker."

"Your what?"

"She makes me do what I've been doing."

Donnie Shoes blinked. He studied Sam in silence for long moments. Then he said, "You got a *chick* that makes you do what you've been doin'."

"I couldn't have said it better myself, but yeah, that's about the whole story in a nutshell."

"And just what does this…Sin…this *chick*…make you do?"

129

"She wants me to go after women. All kinds of women."

"In plain English, asshole."

"Name's Sam. Sam Hughes."

"I don't care *what* the fuck your name is, asshole. You've been fuckin' with me, and when you fuck with me, anyone who knows me will tell you that your name automatically becomes asshole. Or dirtbag. Or shithead. Whatever else you call yourself, I really don't care. When I cap someone who's been fuckin' with me, he becomes fertilizer for the soil, so what do I care *what* the fuck his name is?"

"Sounds a tad harsh."

Donnie Shoes shrugged. "That's what happens when you fuck with me. I'm gonna ask you again, and this time, I wanna know what's goin' on. What exactly does this Sin…this *chick*…make ya do?"

"I'm supposed to nail every babe I come across."

"And *this* is what happened in my club?"

Sam was surprised this man figured it out so quickly. "There ya go. You got it. It's that simple."

Sighing tiredly, Donnie Shoes turned to Flip. "Go find a metal chair and some rope." He pulled a small silver automatic from his jacket pocket and pointed it at Sam. "Me and this asshole, calls himself Sam Hughes, are gonna have a nice, meaningful discussion."

"Sounds cool," Sam said. "What did you want to talk about?"

"Asshole, you're not gonna be able to talk about too much of *anything* when I'm finished with you."

"I take it you don't believe what I said? The Senyllia thing?"

"Do I look stupid, asshole?"

Sam nearly grinned. That sure was an excellent lead-in. But he strongly suspected Donnie Shoes was not the type of dude who enjoyed laughing at himself. Sam had heard a lot of things about mob guys. One thing about them was that they didn't like ridicule. The mere fact that this guy went by the name Donnie Shoes, then turned apeshit when you mentioned his shoes, spoke volumes.

"Well? Do I?" Donnie Shoes repeated.

Sam decided to use a little finesse in this situation.

"Not really," he said. "You've got that low forehead slab-like thing going on, and that one-eyebrow deal does make you look a little witless, but--"

"Flip! Get your ass over here with that shit!"

Sam realized right then that he should have used a little more finesse.

Flip hurried right back, carrying the items. He opened the metal chair and dropped it on the concrete floor, then gestured for Sam to sit in it.

Sam sat.

Flip frantically worked at untangling the loops of clothesline.

Sam figured they were going to do one of their torture things, with Flip doing the nail-pulling or

131

punching or whatever, while Donnie Shoes asked a bunch of stupid questions. Mob guys all seemed to love theatrics. Sam figured that it probably had something to do with their passion for opera.

Sam wondered how they'd react if they shot or stabbed him, and nothing happened.

He decided right then that they wouldn't get the chance. Sam didn't want to be here any longer. These two were keeping him from having a meal before he went back out on the hunt. It wouldn't be long before Senyllia began wondering why he wasn't sending down another thick spray.

"Faster, dammit!" barked Donnie Shoes. The hand holding the gun trembled. Sam could tell Donnie Shoes really wanted to use it.

Flip worked even faster, his thick fingers fumbling with the ropes. When he managed to get a few loops ready, he hurried over to the chair and wrapped one long length around Sam's chest--

Sam raised his head and stared directly at Donnie Shoes.

The man's eyes immediately glazed over. His right arm lowered. His hand relaxed. The pistol clattered to the concrete.

Sam twisted his head around.

Flip, still holding the loops of rope, gawked helplessly at his boss. He jerked his huge head in Sam's direction. "W-What the fuck did you just do to my—"

Sam focused on the big ape.

132

Flip stopped talking. His eyes glazed over. The rope slipped from his hands and dropped quietly to the floor.

Sam got up from the chair and crossed the room. He opened the door and looked out. The three bouncers were standing outside, talking to one another. Two of them were smoking.

Damn. How the hell was he going to sneak past them and get to his car?

Oh well. He'd just have to do the stare thing with them as well.

Before he could slip through the door, blackness enveloped him.

Chapter 13

Donnie Shoes opened his eyes and found himself gawking at an empty chair.

What the fuck?

He vigorously rubbed his eyes. Then he patiently waited for his vision to clear. When it did, he directed his attention once again to the chair.

Still empty. Flip was standing behind it, his face blank, his eyes glazed. Bundles of clothesline lay at his feet.

Donnie suddenly brought up his hands and stared at them. His memory began coming back. When some of the fog lifted, he shifted his gaze. His Sig Sauer lay on the concrete, just two feet from his right shoe.

When did he drop the gun?

What the fuck was going on?

Did he black out?

Still a tad woozy, he struggled to recall the last few minutes.

He'd wanted to cap the bastard but decided to make him squirm a little first. Then he told Flip to find a metal chair and some rope. Flip came back and started unwrapping the rope but wasn't working fast enough

("Faster, dammit!")

to get the job done.

Frustration—as well as anger—threatened to take over. Donnie wanted to knuckle-snap the smartassed bastard for a few minutes before getting some legitimate answers from him. But he couldn't do it because Flip was taking too much damned time to unwrap the rope. Donnie closed his eyes to keep from losing his nut. He promised himself he would not give his damn doctor yet another reason to force him to get off the booze and stay away from the club for a few weeks. What he wanted to do had to be done. The douchebag needed to pay for putting him—as well as the club—through all this. And Donnie would be damned if he let that idiot doctor tell him what to do when this was Donnie's business. After all, who knew better than Donnie Shoes how to run it!

But the problem remained. He was gawking at an empty chair directly in front of him.

Where the fuck had that asshole gone?

Was his high blood pressure doing some nasty tricks to his head?

He had never blacked out before. Even if he had, Flip wouldn't be standing there like that, would he? If Donnie had actually blacked out, Flip would have rushed over and helped. Flip wasn't the brightest bulb in the box, but he wouldn't just stand there like an idiot and watch his boss turn into a fucking *post!*

Blurred images swam sluggishly across his vision. That loud, ass-reaming call from Georgy. Trouble. Threats. Something about Lou Brannon calling, telling Georgy he'd been stiffed by Wendy, saying some idiot had done something screwy to the dancers. First, Wendy, then Nicole.

Donnie had come here because they caught the idiot and brought him here. Three of his best men had brought the asshole here and stood right there next to him, guarding him and making sure he didn't go anywhere. The moron was right here when Donnie came in. And when Donnie came in and saw the dumbass standing there, he promised himself that he was gonna treat himself to a neat little session of knuckle-snapping and facial reassignment.

Just a minute ago, Donnie had told the other three to leave the room so he could have some fun with this asshole. Then, once Donnie and Flip were alone, Donnie ordered Flip to tie that idiot to the chair.

But the damned chair was empty.

And there was no sign of the idiot.

"What the hell just happened?" he asked Flip in a soft voice.

No reply. His eyes glazed, Flip stood totally still. He seemed totally unaware of what was going on.

Donnie walked over and swatted him on the beefy shoulder.

Stiffening, the big boy immediately brought up his hands and held them in front of his face in self-defense. When he realized Donne Shoes was his attacker, he quickly dropped his arms. "Boss? What's goin' on?"

"You tell *me*."

Before Flip could reply, the door opened. Their guns drawn, Vance, Crosley, and Ross rushed in.

136

Vance and Ross stared dumbly at Donnie and Flip while Crosley snuck around Donnie's custom Aston Martin DB5 and Georgy's vintage Rolls. Crosley moved cautiously, his gun held out and ready.

As he watched, Donnie struggled to determine what had just happened. He was certain that his memory hadn't failed him and had just told him exactly what had gone on only moments ago. However, since his men, who had brought that bozo here and held him at gunpoint, were now sneaking around with their guns drawn, he realized that whatever had just happened hadn't been a good thing. But Donnie had already figured that out. The idiot who was supposed to be tied to the metal chair wasn't anywhere to be found. This told Donnie that whatever had just happened was obviously something that just wasn't supposed to make any sense.

"What the fuck's goin' on here?" he asked.

Ross said, "You okay, Boss?"

"I'm fuckin' fine. Now get over it and answer my damn question!"

"Where's that other guy, Boss?" Vance asked.

"What other guy?"

"You *sure* you're okay, Boss?"

"What's with all the stupid questions?"

"There was a guy in here—"

"I remember. A real smartass. Had a thing for my shoes and didn't make much sense whenever I asked him a question. You brought him here, didn't you?"

"Well, yeah, but—"

137

"You didn't let him go, did you?"

"No, sir! No way!"

"Then where the hell *is* he?"

Vance looked clueless.

Donnie turned toward the others. "All of you! Drop what you're doin' right now and listen to me!"

The others instantly straightened and turned to face their boss.

"The dirtbag that did a job on Wendy and Nicole. He should be tied up in that chair right now but he ain't. I don't see him at all. That means either I'm blind or someone fucked up. Since I'm able to see all of you right now, I'll make a quick executive decision and say I'm not blind. This leaves me to believe that other explanation. In other words, one of you fucked up. But since I have a rough idea of how this asshole can get the jump on everyone, I'm not gonna blame any of you for anything he's done. I'm also gonna make it real easy for everyone if ya just tell me what I wanna know." He took a breath and waited for his heart rate to settle down. Then he said, "Where'd he go?"

"Go?" Ross asked.

What the hell was *wrong* with these morons?

"Yeah. *Go*. You know. The opposite of *stay*. He was in here, but he's not anymore. This tells me he ain't here right now." Donnie looked around and shrugged. "*I* don't see him. Do any of *you* see him?"

"Uh, no, Boss—"

"Good. We're all agreed, then. No one sees him. That means if he's not in *here*, he must be

138

somewhere *else*. *That* means if he's somewhere *else*, he had to walk right out that door. There's a back door, but we got stacks of palettes and crates blocking it. If he went out through the front, he woulda had to walk right past the three of *you* bozos."

Silence.

"Anyone have anything to say?"

All four of the men continued looking stupid and ignorant. Donnie wanted to get his camera and take a pic for posterity. He could title it *Dumb, Dumber, Dumbest, Dumbest on Steroids*. He could put it on YouTube for some laughs. He would have, too, if he wasn't so infuriated right now. There was no way that asshole should have been able to get away.

How the hell could *anyone* get past these three without them seeing?

"Weren't you three outside?"

"Yes, sir."

"Yes, sir."

"Yes, sir."

"Weren'tcha watchin' the door?"

Three nods.

"And you didn't see him come outside?"

No reply.

"Talk to me, goddammit. Or I'll fillet *all* your asses right here on the spot!"

Vance said, "We didn't see *anything*, sir."

"You saw *nothin'*?"

No reply.

"C'mon, dammit. I don't have all fuckin' day!"

139

Ross said, "Didn't hear nothin', neither."

"Nothin' *at all*?"

"We don't think so, sir."

Donnie shook his head. This made absolutely no sense whatsoever. "He had to have gone out through that door to make it outside. That's the only damn option I'll consider right now."

"We...didn't *see* him, Boss," Vance said.

"Or hear 'im," Ross added.

"Why not?"

"We...don't know, sir," Crosley muttered uneasily.

"You're tellin' me he just disappeared?"

No reply.

"All three of you are tellin' me that a grown man up and disappeared in front of you."

Three nods.

Flip had said the same thing less than half an hour ago.

He disappeared. The fucker slipped past Flip, took Wendy upstairs, had his way with her, took Nicole outside, had his way with her as well, then disappeared.

And he did the same damn thing here.

No, dammit. It just *couldn't* have happened that way. *No one* could just *disappear*!

"This doesn't make any sense, you know," he told them.

They nodded.

"You're either keepin' somethin' from me or all three of you think you're talkin' to a moron."

140

"We know you're not a moron, Boss," Vance said.

"We *totally* know you're not, Boss," Ross added.

"I'm real glad to know you don't think I'm a moron." Donnie wanted to slap the shit out of all of them.

No one replied. They all gazed at the floor at their feet.

"Then that leaves—"

His cell buzzed. He fished it out of his jacket pocket.

Fuck. It was Georgy.

When the shit came down, it came down in buckets. He might as well drive to the rodeo in Kissimmee, lie down in the center of the arena, and let every single damned horse in the place dump shit all over him.

"Yes, Boss?" he said softly, his voice constricted.

"Talk to me, Dominic. Tell me what's going on in my club."

"Well, Mister D--"

"Dammit, I just had another call, this time from one of my friends, owns half the pawnshops in Kissimmee. Says his son's over there at my place, gettin' taken care of by one of our best girls. The tall blonde. Nicole, I think her name is. The one with the gigantic jugs and huge lips. Anyway, his boy's just about ready to pop, then this dumbass comes right up to her and walks off with her. Just like that!"

141

"Just like with Wendy," Donnie muttered almost to himself.

"Brannon's ready to call in a few favors to find out who's behind all this. Think it's one of those Hispanics that's been givin' us all that trouble?"

Donnie hadn't seriously considered that. It sure as hell made sense. It wouldn't explain how that jerk slipped away from three bouncers standing twenty feet away, but it sure did explain a *few* things. Pete Ramirez, the local boss in Kissimmee, had been giving them grief ever since Georgy bought up the double lot, then had the old building on the place torn down and rebuilt. Ramirez and Georgy gradually developed an understanding and a hands-off policy as a token of mutual respect, but lately Ramirez had been bellyaching about losing money in that section of town and didn't seem to care how vocal he was about it.

"It's a possibility, boss," Donnie said. "Ramirez claims we're stealin' two million a year from him by havin' that place there."

"I've been handing that bastard two percent of the gross ever since just to keep him quiet," Georgy snapped. "That damned fuck obviously wants more."

"Maybe he wants us to up it to five, Boss."

"Five? Just to keep his mouth shut? This could start up something bad."

"I'll talk to him about it, Boss. I need to do it quietly. If it gets out of hand--"

"I know. We could be facing a war. I don't want this to even threaten to head in that direction.

142

Wars are nasty and the wrong people get involved and are hurt or worse. Even if you win, you end up losing."

"I'll see if I can meet with him sometime today."

"See that you do. I'd prefer not to be involved, but if it comes down to it--"

"I understand, Boss."

"Do your best. Let's hope this asshole we want is nothing more than a crazy troublemaker."

Donnie knew better than tell his boss what this "crazy" had said about his "Maker" being a chick and ordering him to nail every babe he came across. For one thing, Georgy was a churchgoer. Like all churchgoers, he was superstitious, and might actually believe they were being jinxed. But Donnie didn't buy into any of that nonsense and saw no reason to bring it up.

"That would be a stroke of luck, wouldn't it?" Donnie said.

"Did you happen to get a glimpse of him?"

"Briefly, Boss." There was no need to tell the man what just happened here.

"Is he Hispanic?"

"I don't think so..."

"Don't matter. He could be freelancing. Spics use non-Spics all the time—especially when they want to make a mess and don't want one of their own caught in the crossfire. But go quietly and carefully. This could turn sloppy in the blink of an eye."

Donnie tried clearing his mind of everything but the face of that bozo. That moron seemed to have more balls than brains—

Call me Sam. My name's Sam Hughes.

Sam Hughes. Was that his *real* name?

What idiot in his right mind causes so much shit, then has the brass *cojones* to give you his real name?

A lunatic.

Otherwise, he wasn't telling Donnie his real name.

Either way, Donnie would find out.

"Boss, I'm gonna make this right."

"See that you do. And Dominic?"

"Yes, Boss?"

"See that this jerk has enough flowers at his funeral. He's a moron, but he might also be a God-fearing moron."

"No problem, Boss."

Chapter 14

"You really *are* a worthless piece of slime, Maggot!"

Daggers shot from Senyllia's eyes, screaming past him before disappearing in the darkness. "A pathetic imbecile! And an extremely grotesque disappointment of mass proportions!"

Sam knelt before her on the hot, clammy ground, wondering what he had done this time. Whatever it was, it sure had her worked up. Her glistening eyes filled their sockets. Steam trickled from every pore of her naked flesh.

He had no idea why she was so pissed. In his view, he had done all that she had expected of him. Since he had made such a huge splash at one of the best-known strip clubs in Central Florida, he thought he would be in the clear.

"Nothing to say?"

"I really don't know why I'm back."

"You have no idea?"

"None."

A groan. "You are *indeed* stupider than I even imagined!"

"What does that have to do with why I'm back?"

"Silence!"

Sam went silent.

"You are back because you opened your mouth about me."

Uh-oh. She had somehow learned what he had told Donnie Shoes. "Oh. That."

"Yes! That!" Angry flame shot out at him, tingling the covering of his spiritual form. Wincing, he gently rubbed his arm and chest.

"Nothing to say?"

"Donnie Shoes wanted to know why I did what I did at his club. I figured that if I told him about you, he'd think I was crazy and would let me go. Then I could go back to hunting down more women. And you'd have more lust juice raining down on you."

"You really *are* an idiot, Samuel Hughes!"

"I guess I am." Now was a good time to find out a few crucial things. "What I don't know is how you found out."

"You really don't know?"

"Nope. I really don't."

She shrugged. "The explanation is simple. Your actions are clearly those of a genuine idiot."

"That's not what I meant."

"Why *did* you mean, then?"

"How did you find out about my telling Donnie Shoes your name?"

She sat up and glared down at him. Her eyes, once again, grew. "I know all and see all. Have you not figured that out yet?"

"I thought…I guess I figured--"

"*What* did you think? *What* did you figure?"

"I never really believed in that know-all crap--"

"And you *still* do not?"

"I guess I do. Now that I've seen it in action."

146

She thought about that for a moment. She appeared to relax somewhat, her huge breasts rising slowly. "Then you are not quite as stupid after all. You belong to me now, Samuel Hughes. You are my servant. My slave. For always. Do you understand what that means?"

"It means that I belong to you? For a long time?"

"Forever."

He was beginning to realize how wrong he had been about this gig. Hell was not actually Heaven at all—not even for a guy like him, and with special powers. And even though he could return to the land of the living and boff any female he chose without suffering the consequences, he wasn't nearly as lucky as he had thought. There were rules to follow. He never enjoyed following rules. Especially when they involved obeying powerful women.

"No comment on that, Samuel Hughes? No snappy witticism?"

"Forever sure is a long, long time," he said uneasily.

"You are trifling with me again..."

"Sorry."

"As I just said, you now belong to me. To put it in simple terms so even an imbecile like you will understand, we are connected. Whatever you do, I will know. Whatever you say, I will know. Whatever you sense or want, I will also know. There is a cord connecting us, and nothing will ever break it."

147

Sam looked down at his feet, then turned around to check behind him.

"It is *invisible*, you idiot!"

He had been correct in his flame idea. It was only a theory at the time, but now he knew for sure. "Is everyone connected to you?"

"*All* my subjects. There are some I no longer worry about, of course. When they have proven to me that they can be trusted, I choose to sever the cord and give them their freedom."

Ah. Hope at last... "Who are they?"

"The ones who have shown intelligence— which is something you obviously need to learn much more about. You haven't earned my trust, Samuel Hughes. I fear you never will."

"Just because I mentioned your name?"

"It is more than that. You have not yet proven you will obey me. You are a womanizer, yet you have failed to dominate every woman you encounter. I am painfully aware of the trouble you experienced with that female outside your tittie club."

"It was no trouble. I got into her car. I let her--
"

"You *hesitated*, Samuel Hughes. You considered ways of getting around it—of *walking away* from her. I popped into your head when you saw her. You wanted to go back in time. You decided to be more selective about where you go, who you look at, who you do not wish to fuck." She shook her head. "You have not joined my team, Samuel Hughes. You have not yet decided to properly satisfy my eternally insatiable lust."

He didn't reply. He saw no need. Now that he was aware of Senyllia's game, he knew how badly he messed up.

"I have already told you I shall be forced to make special arrangements to ensure your cooperation, did I not?"

"Yes, ma'am. You did."

"I am never forced to make alternate adjustments with my *female* subjects--did you know that?"

"No. I didn't."

"Why do you think that is?"

"Females follow orders better than males?"

"They do my bidding because they are *smarter* than males. *That* is the reason."

He definitely did not want to get into that. Male-bashing was one thing. Male-bashing from a huge, ill-tempered female lust demon that shot daggers of fire and didn't seem like a sensible career move.

"I am giving you one last chance."

He didn't know whether this was a good thing, or something else to fear.

"Do not consider this weakness on my part. I have decided to give you one last attempt to redeem yourself only because you carry around the potential I need to remain constantly satisfied."

"Potential?"

149

"You are obsessed with sex. All my subjects are. They *have* to be. Otherwise, I do not want them around."

"So there *is* hope for me, then?"

"As I have just said, you have been given one last chance. One. And one only."

He waited nervously for her proposition.

"You will follow my orders exactly, from now on, Samuel Hughes. If you do not, if you somehow decide to return to your former idiocy, I will pull you to back to Hell and you will remain here. Forever. And I will be sure to hand you over to one of the other demons."

"Bummer..."

"What was that?"

"I said I understand."

Her arm lashed out. Large tongues of flame shot at him. He gritted his teeth, closed his eyes, and waited for the searing surge to end. He knew it would only last a few seconds, but it was excruciatingly painful. He could barely breathe as the flames and the smoke encircled him, pressing against his face, smothering him.

Then it was gone.

When the flames vanished, he collapsed.

"Samuel Hughes?"

Panting, he pushed himself up and squinted in her direction.

She was watching him curiously. She seemed to be looking at him differently. The anger had left her face.

He groaned. "Wow. That hurt like hell!"

"I put an extra pang into that one." She sounded proud.

"What the hell *was* that?"

"You shall soon see."

"You mean, you did something to me again? Something different?"

She shrugged. "You have given me no other choice, Samuel Hughes."

"W-What did you do?"

"You shall find out shortly."

"Oh boy..." The glint in her eyes frightened him.

"Would you prefer to become a plaything for one of the other demons? I understand one of them is looking for something he can turn into a basketball."

She had to be kidding. "Really?"

"As a mortal, this demon was a professional athlete. I have heard that he has fashioned several basketball hoops from the rotting jawbones of condemned politicians and would like something to toss at them during periods of boredom." She shook her head. "Anyway, if you would like to become his personal basketball, the job is open."

"Thanks, but I think I'll pass on that one."

"This is good. We are both satisfied, then?"

"In a manner of speaking."

She blinked. "Are you satisfied that you will soon be leaving this place or not?"

"Yes. Definitely. Totally."

"You have also learned a valuable lesson during this last visit, did you not?"

"I sure did."

"And just what would this lesson be?"

He had hoped she wouldn't ask him something like that. His mind reeled, but the fear of her powers fueled his thought processes, quickly producing something that would probably sound reasonable. "I shouldn't have opened my big mouth about you."

"Excellent." She sounded pleased. "What else?"

Once again, his thoughts looped chaotically, filling his head with images. *Sex*, it told him. *She craves lust—lots of it. Constantly.* "I'll never again hesitate about having sex with anyone again."

"No. You will not."

The way she responded—as well as the obvious victory showing in her eyes—made him both suspicious and frightened.

"Let me put it this way, Samuel Hughes. You will never find yourself in the position to hesitate again."

What the hell does she mean by that?

Despite the intense heat surrounding him, chills trickled down his spine. She had sounded very sinister just then. The gleam in her eye turned his spirit icy cold.

But he knew better than voice his concerns.

Senyllia suddenly smiled. "I do not think I will have any problems from you again, will I?"

"No, ma'am. No problems at all. None."

"Good-bye, Samuel Hughes. I am incredibly pleased that this last meeting was much more productive than the others."

"I think so, too." He knew he was much better off, agreeing with her. He didn't want more flame burning into him. And he certainly didn't want her turning him into an insect again. "In fact—"

Blackness.

He woke up on the gravel beside his Camaro.

He sat up and checked his surroundings. The front lot of Georgy's Girls Galore. Some cars pulled out while others turned in off the main road. The two gorillas stood out front, as usual.

But this time, no one was after him. In fact, no one even glanced in his direction.

Good deal. He had managed to survive another traumatic experience.

He pulled open the door, slid behind the wheel, and started up the engine. He was groggy from his latest experience with Senyllia, but it was no big deal. He could manage.

He had escaped Hell again. And he had done it in one piece.

When he got back to the apartment, he would celebrate.

Then it would be wise to take some time off to recuperate.

Chapter 15

Philip "Flip" Aaronson pulled Donnie Shoes' black BMW into the front entrance of the apartment complex and eased down the winding gravel path.

Bob Vance sat beside him while Al Crosley and Carl Ross occupied the back seat. When Flip passed the unit marked K12, he continued coaxing the luxury ride down the straight stretch leading to the complex pool and tennis courts. He pulled into a vacant visitor's spot facing a small stucco building marked *Clubhouse*.

"Sure it's K twelve?" Vance asked.

Flip flicked off the ignition. He reached inside his jacket and pulled out his Sig Sauer from the Uncle Mike's holster beneath his huge left arm. "Course it's K twelve. It's what my connection at DMV said."

"I dunno about this." Vance squirmed in the seat.

Flip didn't like it when one of the guys lost his nerve. This was necessary and they all knew it. You just didn't mess with Donnie Shoes or Big Georgy. If shit like that got around, every dumbass in the damned state would make life miserable for *everyone*.

"What the fuck don't you know?" Flip checked the magazine and slipped the gun back into its holster. "The asshole fuckin' with Donnie and the rest of us lives here. We go in, bring him back out,

154

and take him back to Donnie. Short and simple. To me, anyway…"

"Sucks," Vance said.

"We've done shit like this before," Flip said. "What's got your panties in a knot?"

"Simple. We gotta bring him in alive."

"No problem." Flip shrugged. "He wants to get frisky? We clip him in the back of the neck. Crosley also brought knockout juice with him. Right, Croz?"

"Don't like usin' it, though," Crosley said. "He pissed us off. I might give 'im too much accidentally on purpose."

"So?"

"Too much might kill him."

"Then we tell Donnie our bozo had a little accident."

"Donnie wants 'im for himself," Vance said. "We fuck up, Donnie'll eat us alive."

"We'll be careful," Ross said. "Like Flip just said, we've done this before."

"This is different." Vance sounded spooked.

"What's different about it?"

"Him."

"Who?"

"Dude we're goin' after. Hughes. Still can't figure what he did back there at the warehouse."

"No one can fuckin' disappear," Ross said almost to himself.

"He didn't disappear." Crosley shook his head. But he sounded doubtful.

"If he didn't disappear," Vance said, "how the hell did he get past us?"

Silence.

"I wasn't out there," Flip said. "I was inside with Donnie. But I'll bet that asshole came back. I'll bet he didn't set foot outside."

"You don't know for sure?"

Flip wasn't sure of anything. All he knew was that Hughes had somehow suckered him twice. That really ticked him off, and he promised himself there wouldn't be a third time.

"What were *you* doin'?" Crosley asked. "Strokin' your dick?"

"I...don't *know* what the fuck I was doin'," Flip said, sighing. "It's all fuzzy."

Vance shivered. "This is what's spookin' the tits off me."

"He *musta* come back in," Ross said.

"Impossible," Flip said.

"He came back in and waited, prob'ly behind Georgy's Rolls, since it's so damn big. Then he snuck back out soon as we rushed in." Ross shrugged.

"We weren't lookin' anywhere else," Crosley said after some thought. "We were starin' at the fuckin' *door*."

"He disappeared." Vance's voice was a whisper. "I don't know how, I just know he did, because that's the only thing that makes any damn sense."

"*No one* can fuckin' disappear," Ross said again, frowning.

156

"He *must* have if he got past you and Donnie," Vance said. "How else could he even get to the door?"

Flip didn't say anything for a while. Then, after a deep sigh, he said, "He suckered us. I don't know how, he just did. And he's gonna tell us how, soon as we find him and haul his ass back to Donnie."

"How the fuck could he sucker all *five* of us?"

"How the fuck should *I* know?" Flip found that he was getting even angrier. "I told ya, everything went fuzzy, dammit. He's some sort of magician, I figure. Fucker musta hypnotized us or something."

"*Both* of you?"

Flip rubbed the back of his thick columnar neck. "No, brainiac. Donnie *let* him get away. He felt *sorry* for him. Said he reminded him of his *mother*." He shot a glare at the three of them. "Of *course, both* of us!"

"Think he actually *hypnotized* ya?" Crosley asked.

"How else could he get away?"

"He didn't have any stuff with him?"

"Stuff?"

Crosley shrugged. "Magic powder, somethin' just like it. Magician dudes always have weird shit in their pockets. When they want to slip somethin' past ya, they toss it in your face. You don't even know they did it, 'cause it zaps ya for a second. Just long enough to let them get away. And when ya open your eyes and see somethin' different, ya think they actually did hit ya with magic."

"Sounds like a crock to me."

"Ninjas do that." Ross nodded.

"Do what?"

"Use some weird ancient powder."

"They got to," Crosley said. "Otherwise, they can't do any of that neat shit. It's why people think Ninjas are magical beings. They can disappear in the middle of a fight, circle around their opponent, slice their head off, then disappear again."

Flip wasn't convinced. He kept telling himself that there was no reason for these guys to fear the bozo. "This Hughes moron isn't magical, dammit!"

"How can ya say that?"

"He's not a Ninja, for one thing."

"How do ya know?"

"Ninjas are usually Asians."

"Steven Seagal isn't Asian."

"He also ain't human. Anyway, he ain't no Ninja."

"Good point. Maybe Sam Hughes ain't human, either."

"He's human, but he's no Ninja."

"Well, if he's human and not a Ninja, what the fuck *is* he? No normal guy can slip past five guys without any of 'em seeing 'im."

"Sam Hughes is just an asshole."

"Course he's an asshole. He's also pretty damn smart."

"Still think it was a trick."

"If it was," Flip said, "I'd love to know how he did it."

"Why?"

158

"Next time Donnie Shoes wants to ream me a new one, I'll just work him like Hughes and go get a thick, juicy steak. Then I'll come back when I think Donnie's finished and act like I hadn't budged."

"Sounds ridiculous," Crosley said.

"No more ridiculous than your magic theory."

"Anybody here got *any* ideas about this shit?" Vance said.

Ross nodded. "If *I* did, I'd sure as hell—"

"Guys." Flip held up his hand. Down the road to their left, the familiar figure got out of a green Camaro, crossed the walk, and went into Unit K12. "It's Hughes. He's now up for grabs. Let's rock."

***

Tired from an excruciatingly long, hectic day, Sam stepped into the living room of his apartment.

The place looked the same and felt the same, but after his latest trip from Hell, everything seemed different. New. Fresh. Untouched. Even the outside air seemed fresher. He suddenly had the urge to smell the flowers in his neighbor's front yard but realized how weird that would be.

It was time to get out of his soiled clothes. He'd been wearing them all day and desperately needed a shower.

He stood beneath the heavy warm spray for ten minutes. After toweling down, he blow-dried his hair and went into the bedroom for a change of clothes.

He put on a fresh pair of undershorts, an old pair of frayed jeans that had been cut off just above

159

the knee, and a red tee shirt. Then he went back to the bathroom, combed his hair, and brushed his teeth.

After fixing dinner, he planned to head on out to the pool and check out the late afternoon activities. Or maybe mosey on over to the tennis court, where a couple of young babes teaching at the local college liked shedding some extra weekend calories. One of them, a skinny blonde, came out regularly and even spent some time in the pool. Looked good, too. There were also a couple of other babes who lounged around the pool on the weekends, working on their tan. He figured them for lesbians but couldn't really be sure. One of his lifelong fantasies had always been having sex with two babes. Maybe he could check them out one of these days. Since he had powers, he didn't think he'd have a problem conning them into bed.

In any event, he planned to explore the premises a little later and see who he could gratify for the evening.

Once he was satisfied that his hair looked good enough, he left the bathroom and went down the hall.

And froze.

Four huge men stood in the living room, blocking the door.

All pointed guns at him.

He recognized them instantly. The bouncers from the club. Three of them were the goons he encountered in the warehouse. The fourth was the human tank named Flip, who he had suckered on

160

his way to the Platinum Room, as well as in their warehouse.

The only one missing was Donnie Shoes.

Flip was scowling and peering down the hall. "Where the fuck is he?"

"Pardon me?"

"You heard him," the one beside Flip said. "We saw 'im come in here not ten minutes ago. We been waitin' outside—just in case he spotted us and slipped out. We know damn well that he didn't. So…where the hell is he?"

What were they talking about? Sam was the only one here. He was the one they were looking for. And they were looking right at him.

Something was seriously weird. The way these guys were staring at him made him extremely uncomfortable.

Flip said, "Keep 'er here, Vance. Ross and Croz, you come with me to look for the bastard."

One of them said, "Looks like a one-bedroom. Should only take a minute."

The one called Vance motioned with his gun. "C'mere, bitch. Stay out of the way and you won't get hurt."

Her?

Bitch?

What the hell was going on?

"You guys all right?" he asked. "I mean--"

"Shuddup," Vance said. "Just get the fuck over here and stay quiet till we find where you're hidin' the bozo."

161

Sam slipped carefully around the corner and stood in front of the two barstools at the kitchen counter. The others rushed right past as they went down the hall.

"Hiding who? And why did you just call me *bitch*?"

Vance looked him up and down. "You're really one hot babe, bitch…" He shook his head. "That asshole sure must have somethin' extra."

Sam looked down at himself.

Nothing different.

What the hell were they talking about?

Her? Hot? Babe? Bitch?

And the others had just sprinted down the hall, looking for him. But why look for him when he was standing right here?

The other three came right back. Flip walked over and stopped less than a foot from him. Sam found himself staring at the man's mammoth chest. "You got one chance and one chance only to tell us where the fuck Sam Hughes is, lady."

"I have no idea what you're talking about, guys. If this is a stupid game--"

"We don't play games, bitch," said another angrily. "If you don't tell us what we wanna know, we're gonna have to do some nasty things to find out where that moron is."

Sam no longer thought this was some sort of weird game. These guys looked serious. Worse, they looked extremely angry.

"I really don't understand what's going on. And why do you keep calling me bitch?"

"Listen here," Flip said. "We saw that bozo Hughes drive up in his Camaro. We saw the same bozo park right outside the door. We even saw this same bozo get out and come into this apartment."

"You're absolutely right."

"We know we're right. I told ya, we saw 'im come in. But you know what? Somethin' else happened that's very puzzlin' to us right now."

He was afraid to ask. He just shrugged.

"We didn't see 'im come back out."

This was way the hell past strange. He had suspected these goons were stupid but didn't think anyone could be as stupid as they were acting now. How could someone forget your face so quickly?

"You really didn't see him come back out?" he asked curiously.

Vance shook his head and moved closer. "Ya know damn well we didn't. Care to explain that?"

There was no sense being scared anymore. He was dead, wasn't he? They couldn't kill him. The worst they could do was torture him like they did in the movies. But he still had the edge. He could probably piss them off enough to get them to shoot him. Then he could wait until they left or dumped his body, then clean himself up, leave, and go back out to look for strange stuff again.

"I think I just might be able to," he said.

Flip was still scowling. "We were hopin' ya could. See, we just checked out this apartment, top to bottom. Thing is, there's only one door. And the only window that opens—aside from the livin' room and dinin' room—is in the bedroom. But we

163

don't think he used it. We don't think *anyone* can use it. It's got a damn screen. Anyone tries to slip out, they'd have to take out the screen. Bozo coulda pulled it out, slipped outside, then had you put it back, but we don't think that happened. One of us woulda seen him come out. Like I said, we been watchin' this place ever since he came inside."

This was getting *so* out of hand. Sam had no idea what was going on. They were standing around him, looking right at him, yet they had no idea where he was. They could not have forgotten his face so soon.

Worse, they were talking to him as if he were a female.

Were they in some sort of trance? He didn't think so. They seemed totally in control.

So then, if they weren't in a trance, what the hell was happening?

Maybe he *hadn't* come back from Hell. Maybe he was still in transit—or whatever it was called when you were moving between two worlds. Or maybe *he* was the one in the trance. That last encounter with Senyllia had been unusually rough.

That's the only thing that could have happened. He was imagining all this.

Or at least some of it.

He had to look at himself, make sure he was all right. He realized right then that he could be suffering from a concussion. He could have hit his head during that last fall down below.

"I need to step into the bathroom, if you guys don't mind."

164

"Gotta pee?"

"I feel a little faint. I need to splash my face with some cold water."

"Sure. Go ahead. But we'll go with you—if ya don't mind."

"No problem." He made a move toward the hall. He thought they'd give him a rough time, but they didn't stop him. So far, so good. Just a quick check in the mirror and he'd be fine.

Nothing had seemed different while he was brushing his teeth and drying his hair. But something strange *had* happened, possibly within the last five minutes. And it must have taken place just moments before they came in.

He hurried down the hall, slipped into the bathroom, and flicked on the light.

And found himself staring at his reflection.

Nothing out of the ordinary. Nothing different. No circles, no bruises. His pupils weren't dilated. It was him. Sam Hughes. He appeared no different. The same eyes, face, and hair.

The important thing was that he was himself. A guy. Man. Male.

So…what the hell were these goons talking about?

"Ain'tcha gonna splash your face?" one of them asked.

"I've changed my mind."

"All right, then." Flip moved closer. "What's your explanation, lady?"

Flip stood on Sam's right, Vance on his left. Sam felt small, insignificant, and powerless.

But most of all, he could feel the sheer terror building within him.

The realization of the situation made him weak at the knees.

These three obviously thought he was a female. They actually *saw* him as a *woman*.

But why?

"Guys, I know you're not gonna believe this--"

"Try us."

"I'm Sam Hughes."

The three of them exchanged strange glances, then laughed.

Vance spoke first. "Good disguise, bitch. Real good."

"It's *not* a disguise!"

"What is it, then?" Flip asked.

How the hell was he supposed to answer? *You guys are all crazy? You're obviously hallucinating because you're looking at a guy and thinking I'm a female? I'm not a lady? I'm male? A guy? I've got a dick, just like you?*

The only thing he knew was the truth. There was no way he could lie his way out of this. "I'm trying to *tell* you, I'm *Sam Hughes!*"

"You're full of shit. You're one really hot-looking babe, but you're still full of shit."

"*Real* hot," commented Vance softly, gazing at Sam's chest.

Ross was standing out in the hall, staring at him as well. He sighed and shook his head. "How come all the hottest babes have to be batshit crazy?"

166

Flip shrugged. "I think that comes with the territory when ya gotta deal with horny guys all the time."

"I'm *not a female!*" Sam could clearly feel the panic settling in.

"All right, all right. You're not a female. Show us."

"*Huh*?"

"Take off your clothes."

Senyllia. The damned bitch had done something.

Now he understood. Dammit, it had to be the flame thing. She had slammed him with some strange, horrible spell.

You will never find yourself in the position to hesitate again...

My God. Now it was plain and simple.

The demon bitch had made it so nothing he ever said or did from now on would help him.

Sam's pulse raced. He had no idea what to do. If he took off his clothes and appeared to them as a female, he was toast, plain and simple. He knew what guys were like when a female pissed them off—especially if she was naked, and even worse if she was hot, as they had just said. And infinitely worse if there were more than one of them, and they were all revved up.

But he didn't have much choice.

"Listen. I know you won't believe this, but--"

"Take it *all* off, baby."

"But I'm really a *guy*--"

"Off!"

167

"The truth is, I'm not really here. I'm actually dead, and--"

"Guess she's even crazier as we thought."

"With that body, she can be as crazy as a bedbug, for all I care!"

"Guess she needs a little help with her clothes."

"I volunteer."

"Me, too!"

"I get the cut-offs!"

Before Sam could react, the four of them yanked off his tee shirt and shoved down his shorts and briefs, until his chest and privates showed in full view.

They all stood back and stared. Sam could feel the tension growing in the room. Two of them swallowed. Flip began breathing more rapidly. Both Vance and Ross had their mouths wide-open. Drool had gathered on their lower lips.

"What's next, bitch?" Flip asked. "You gonna tell us that ain't a *pussy* we're lookin' at?"

"Or tits?"

"Oh boy," Crosley whispered, rubbing his jeans.

"Me, too."

"Nice stuff!"

"Think Hughes would mind?"

"Who gives a shit? He left her here, didn't he?"

"Stupid fuck."

"Who in his right mind would leave such a hot-looking babe alone with four horny guys?"

"Hughes really *is* a stupid dick."

168

Sam opened his mouth, but nothing came out.

They picked him up and carried him into the bedroom. He tried resisting at first and was rewarded with a harsh slap to the jaw. He was so weak with fear, he just let them toss him on the bed. He lay there helplessly, watching them numbly as they frantically yanked off their clothes.

Panic rocked through him. His heart thrashed wildly. His flesh had turned to ice.

If only they would just shoot him and leave him lying here...

This was much worse. Worse than death. Worse, even, than facing Senyllia again.

He struggled to breathe, then forced himself to think, to use his head. To gather up anything he could find. Anything that might sound like words.

After another mighty breath, his thoughts finally came out in a torrent. "Guys? This is all a big *mistake*! You don't know what you're *doing*! *Please*! Don't *do* this! I'm Sam Hughes! I'm a *guy*! I swear to God--"

For the next hour, the boys took turns pounding him senseless. As two of them gripped Sam's ankles tightly, keeping his legs spread wide, a third slammed brutally into him while another straddled Sam's shoulders and shoved his swollen shaft down Sam's throat.

Finally, after praying for unconsciousness to rescue him from this horror, Sam mercifully passed out.

Chapter 16

Sam opened his eyes to the semi-darkness.

My God. I've returned to Hell. I'm back, this time to stay.

However, something was different. This didn't have the feel of Hell. Or the smell. There was no eye-watering sulphurous reek, for one thing. And the darkness wasn't foul or fathomless.

He turned his head. About ten feet away, slender horizontal beams of light seeped through the blinds of a small window, piercing the darkness.

This definitely was not Hell. He didn't remember seeing *any* windows down there.

Also, there was no strong almond odor.

And he wasn't lying in hot mud.

It was a mattress. He was lying under a sheet. In a single bed.

He sat up. Dizziness overtook him, forcing him to lie back down.

His body throbbed with pain. Red marks covered his wrists. His ankles also throbbed, telling him they carried similar marks. His jaw ached, bringing back the sharp image of what had happened. He forced his mind away from that horror. His pelvis felt as if he had been run over by something huge and extremely heavy. His ass pulsated as if it had been rammed with a baseball bat.

His blurred vision frightened him. He gently felt his left cheekbone. It was swollen and hurt like the blazes.

He had been pummeled, mauled, and abused. And judging by his memories of what had happened in his apartment, he considered himself fortunate that the blackness had knocked him out so quickly.

But where was he right now?

Where had those thugs brought him?

This was obviously someone's apartment. The cheap furniture, the musty smell, the blinds covering the single window, and the well-worn armchair---everything attested to this. He had seen a similar room before but could not remember the details. Or anything else about it. Not now, anyway. The cloudiness in his head refused to clear.

Had they brought him here once they had finished with him?

Where was he? And why was he here?

Most important, *who* was he?

His name was Sam Hughes, and he was a *man*—not a *woman*. No matter how much he had infuriated Senyllia, how much he had disappointed her, she couldn't possibly have the power to change him into a woman.

Or *could* she?

He recalled her frequent bursts of violent temper, the sparks flying from her eyes, her mouth. The flame oozing from her. She was a damned powerful demon, all right. In fact, she was downright terrifying.

But could she actually *change* his sex?

171

No. She could not. She would not.

Taking a breath, he brought up his arms. They weighed a ton, but he forced himself to continue. He needed them to check himself out. It was important to make sure that he hadn't changed, that his body remained the same.

Taking a deep breath, he forced himself to pull the sheet away.

He was totally naked.

He sighed in relief. The same chest. The same genitals.

He had never realized how wonderful it was to look down at himself.

He was still a man. He was born a man and had died a man. No one could change that.

Yet, because of Senyllia and her disgusting spell, no one else *knew* he was a man.

Senyllia, if you have any decency...

He almost laughed aloud.

A *demon* having *decency*? *That* was one for the ages.

But this sort of desperation brought about an almost childlike sense of hope.

This was a dream—nothing more, nothing less. A very bad, twisted dream brought on by Senyllia and his repeated trips to Hell.

Yet, some terrible darkness lurking in the back of his mind told him otherwise.

The door opened.

A slender young woman with thick red hair and large breasts came in, carrying a small tray. She looked very familiar. She wore a black sleeveless tank top and tight frayed jeans. Open-toed white sandals covered her feet. She pushed the door shut with a slight jerk of her hip and placed the tray on the small table in the corner.

"You're up," she said, moving closer to the bed.

"I guess I am," Sam said. "More or less."

"I'm Wendy."

Oh my God. She was the dancer he had taken out of the Platinum Room. The babe he had tied to the bed and attacked over and over, for more than an hour.

Was this the same room he had brought her to?

Hardly. The table in that room was covered with an assortment of S&M instruments. He suspected this could be the same building.

"Uh...hi..." He found it difficult to look her in the face. The guilt was already nipping at him. He had left her spread-eagled naked to the bed, her head covered with a submission helmet, a ring gag filling her mouth, his juice streaking her cheeks and chin.

Very humiliating, to say the least.

She smiled. "Well? What do I call *you*?"

"I'm...Sam..."

"Short for Samantha?"

"Just call me Sam." He was much too tired and overwhelmed with fear, remorse, and confusion to waste energy explaining. "Where am I?"

A shrug. "The club--where else?"

"The *club*?"

173

"Gals Galore. On the Trail. One of Big Georgy's places. We're upstairs. Donnie told us to look in on you."

"Donnie?"

"Our boss."

Donnie Shoes. *My God...* The images swam past his vision, jolting him fully alert.

He rubbed his temples and forced the harsh memories aside. He had to clear his head. It was time to find out what was happening, and he had to do it right now, while he still retained *some* of his senses.

"Why...am I here?"

She shrugged. "I just told you. You were brought in."

"By who?"

"I really don't know. They don't tell us girls anything, actually. Donnie just told us to look in on you." She frowned. "You don't remember *anything*?"

"No. Nothing."

"Water?"

"Huh?"

"Would you like a glass of water? You're probably thirsty."

"Thanks. I am."

"You oughta be. You looked pretty bad when they brought you in."

He was afraid to ask. "When...was that?"

"Yesterday afternoon." Her brows mashed together. "Are you *sure* you don't remember?"

A full day gone. Gone and forgotten. But it shouldn't matter, should it? He was dead. He shouldn't even care about the days anymore. Or the nights. Or anything else.

Wendy picked up a glass from the tray, came over, and handed it to him.

He drank the water and frowned. Bitter. Tap water, obviously. But it was better than nothing. He drank nearly the whole glass. His throat was sore and raspy. He didn't even want to remember what had been forced down there. The cool liquid worked wonders.

Wendy sat down in the chair beside the bed. She seemed to be taking inventory. "So…you're the girlfriend."

"What?"

"The guy who really pissed off Donnie Shoes. And me. And Nicole. And just about all the bouncers at the club. You're his girl."

His girl.

Senyllia, you bitch!

The horrible images filled his head. His apartment. The bathroom. Studying himself in the mirror, then taking off his clothes and noticing nothing different. The four bouncers watching him. Drooling. Rubbing their crotches. Grinning lecherously. Then picking him up and--

Stop it. Focus.

"Is *that* why I'm here?"

Wendy looked confused. "Why do you think?"

"Like you said, I was kinda out of it."

Wendy stared at his wrists and nodded. "I see that. Donnie's boys can be rough. You must've pissed them off when you didn't tell them what they wanted to know."

"Their being pissed off wasn't what concerned me at the time."

Wendy reached out and patted his shoulder. "Can't blame 'em, can we, Sam?" She tilted her head and giggled. "How 'bout that? Sam and Sam. If he wasn't such a jerk, I'd think that was really cute."

"That's why we hooked up," he said curtly. "We thought it would look good on personalized Christmas cards. Why can't we blame them?"

Wendy's eyes grew. "Look at you. You're gorgeous."

Gorgeous? I'm gorgeous?

Senyllia had made him *gorgeous?*

Why, of course she would. For her repulsive plan to work, Sam would have to be dazzling. Stunning. Irresistible. Otherwise, no one would want him. There would be no challenge. And if there was no challenge, there would be no sex.

I wouldn't have to worry about every guy I stumble across wanting to jump my bones...

"So I'm gorgeous. This lets them do whatever they want?" he asked.

She shrugged a shoulder. "They're *guys*, sweetie. We all know what guys are like, don't we? Especially when they get together in a pack."

A pack. That surely was an appropriate term.

"Yeah. We all know."

176

"But it's really not *that* bad, is it?"

How could she say such a thing?

He stared at her expression and wondered if she realized what she had just said. "You do know what they did, don't you?"

She appeared to be thinking it over. "I *sort of* have an idea--"

"They raped me. All four of them. Over and over." The heat sliced through him as he said it.

She patted his arm and sighed. "I'm sorry, honey. I didn't know it was that bad."

"Yeah. It was that bad."

"Was that your first time?"

Was she serious? "For what?"

"Listen, I know it was bad, but what I meant was, it coulda been worse."

"How?"

"You survived, didn't you?"

"Yeah, I guess I did." No reason to tell her otherwise. It would probably make her think he was crazy. "How does that make this any better?"

"It doesn't—not really."

"Then why'd you say it?"

She sighed. "Honey, you can use this if you know how to use it on the right people. You just use it to get exactly what you want."

"*Use* it?"

"Your looks, baby. You know what I'm talking about." She laughed and swatted him lightly on the shoulder. "For a moment, you had me going."

"Blame it on my head. It's still kinda foggy."

"I understand. But you know what I mean. You work in a place like this, you can have your pick. Once you belong to someone or a small group, no one else is allowed to touch you. And you can make money—lots of it."

He tried a gamble. "Is *that* why I'm here?"

"Can you dance?"

"I never really tried."

"In a place like this, you don't have to be a professional, if you know what I mean. All you really have to do is look good naked and know how to move around to get the customers turned on. And believe me, that's not that hard at all, because they're turned on even before they come into this place. In other words, it doesn't really take much to get them off. Just look good, move around a lot, show as much skin as you can, and make sure you bend over once in a while, to show off your butt and those boobs. You look good, baby. From what I can see, you're perfect. How old are you?"

"Thirty-two."

"Really? Ya look more like twenty-five. Nature's been good to you."

Senyllia obviously did helluva job.

"We always got along," he replied.

"How's that?"

"Me and nature. I never litter, dump chemicals, or chop down trees."

Wendy laughed. "You're funny, Sam. These guys'll like that. Anyway, once those bruises heal, you'll look fabulous." She shrugged. "But don't worry about the dancing. Donnie'll pay one of us to

178

teach a new girl the moves if she's gorgeous. I'm sure he'll have one of us work with you."

Sam didn't reply. He was trying to fully understand what had really happened in the last twenty-four hours.

"None of this would've happened to you if they had found your boyfriend," Wendy said.

"How do you figure?"

"Donnie's an okay guy to work for, but he's one of those hard-headed Italians who goes crazy when someone messes with him. He really wanted to find your boyfriend. Face it, that guy of yours pulled some serious boners here the other day. And since Donnie couldn't find him..." She shrugged. "I guess you're the next best thing. He didn't want his boys to come back empty-handed."

"That makes me feel *so* much better."

"Those are the breaks, I guess. But like I said, it coulda turned out much worse. This is a really great place to work. They treat you well and pay you well. You can build a nice, fat nest egg here if you work it just right."

Terrific. A nice, fat nest egg. And all he had to do was dance naked in front of a bunch of horny men and let a few of them rape him every night.

"Listen. Wendy. This is all a terrible mistake--"

"How long were you with that Sam guy?"

"Not long."

"I figured as much."

"How's that?"

"He didn't stick around."

179

"Huh?"

"He threw you under the bus and just disappeared. If he had cared about you at all, he wouldn't have done that."

"I'm sure he had his reasons."

Wendy shook her head. "You were much too good for him, honey."

"You didn't know him."

Wendy's dark-blue eyes suddenly blazed. "He brought me up here in the middle of my spot, made me give him a hummer, then tied me to the bed. He fucked me over and over, until he got bored. Then he just left me there, tied to the bed with a ring gag in my mouth and his cum all over my face." She took a breath and shook her head. "And now you're *defending* him?"

Sam just shrugged. There wasn't much he could say. He felt really bad for what he'd done to this babe. Wendy was very sweet. If it hadn't been for Senyllia, he would never have treated her like that. But he knew that no matter how bad you felt about some things, you just couldn't undo the past. He was just relieved that she had no idea who he really was.

"Do you know why he did that?" Wendy asked.

"Why he tied you to the bed?"

"Why he cheated on you."

"I guess it's one of those guy things."

Wendy frowned. "Guys like him really piss me off. But I'm glad they went after him. At least he knows how badly he messed up. He also knows

180

what'll happen if he shows his face in this town again."

"Oh, I don't think we'll be seeing him again," Sam said sourly.

"If he's smart, he won't *ever* show his face around here." Wendy patted his shoulder. "You're lucky to be rid of him."

"Yeah. Rid of Sam and now I'm here."

"Oh, don't worry about Flip and the others. Now that you're under contract, they won't touch you again. You're Donnie's property, and that makes you hands-off. All of us are."

"Contract?"

"It's usually for two years, but if someone really important likes you, he'll buy your contract from Donnie and take you out of here. But if you want to stay here, your guy will make some sort of exclusive arrangement with Donnie so he's the only one you'll ever have to perform for. It's like the one Lou Brannon has with me. Nicole also has one of those, and four other girls. Don't worry, Sam. You'll do really well here. And no one'll even bother with--"

"I'm...not a *woman*," he said flatly. He didn't know why he said it. It didn't seem to matter anymore. But it was the only thing that still made sense. The only thing keeping him from going insane.

"How's that, honey?"

"I said, I'm not a woman."

She didn't reply.

He took a deep breath and let it come out. "I'm a man...trapped in a woman's body!"

Wendy laughed. "You really are funny, Sam. You'll be a great hit with these guys. They *like* us to have a sense of humor. It loosens 'em up, makes 'em spend more--"

"I'm serious. I'm not a real woman."

She winked and patted his arm. "I get it."

"You do?"

"Sure. We've all got our problems. Mine? I always end up falling for the wrong guy. It's why I'm here in the first place. There was this guy--"

"I'm a *guy*, dammit! A *guy*! Can't you *see* that?" He tossed the sheet away and grabbed his dick. He shook it at her. "What's *this* look like? You can't shake a *pussy*, can you? It's a *dick*! A *cock*! Can't you tell?" He cupped his balls with his other hand. "And these! Look at these! They're *balls*, angel. *Testicles*! Don't tell me you haven't seen a shitload of *these* before..."

Wendy squinted at him. "You okay, honey? I can tell they knocked ya around quite a bit. That eye looks kinda ouchy, but--"

"Listen to this." Sam swatted his chest with a fist. It made a loud thumping sound in the room. "Does this *look* or *sound* like a woman's chest?"

"Honey, I think you need more rest. I really do. In fact--"

A knock on the door.

Wendy jumped up and crossed the room. She opened the door, stuck her head through the small gap, and mumbled something to whoever was out in

182

the hall. She closed the door and hurried back to Sam. "Gotta go, honey. You've got business right now."

"But--"

"I brought you a sandwich. For later." She gestured to the tray. "It's nothing special, just ham and cheese on rye with some pretzels and chips. I also added a few carrot sticks and some Ranch dressing—in case you like that kind of stuff. We figured you'd be hungry."

"Wendy." His heart thumped. He didn't want to be here. Or watch her leave. Or be in this room when the door opened, and some other horror leaped into this frightening new life.

"Later, honey." She waved, then rushed out of the room.

The window. Maybe he could force it open and escape *that* way...

His pulse raced as he forced himself out of bed. Ignoring the protests of his aching joints and bruises, he searched frantically for his clothes.

He quickly found that they were nowhere in the room.

A red robe lay in a wrinkled heap on the floor in front of the armchair. He picked it up and squirmed into it. It was slightly big but would suffice.

Now...if he could only get that damned window open wide enough for him to—

The door opened abruptly.

Donnie Shoes came in and closed the door softly behind him.

183

Dressed in a tan, tailor-fitted two-piece suit, blood red tie, and brown suede shoes, he stared directly at Sam. His expression showed intense curiosity.

Sam could tell he was being carefully evaluated. He moved over to the bed and tied his robe shut before sitting.

Donnie Shoes lowered his large butt into the armchair. "You don't look *too* bad. Couple weeks, mebbe, for that shiner. The fat lip'll be okay in a few days. No biggie."

"Thanks. I feel just great."

Donnie shrugged. "Those boys usually know how to behave. You musta agitated 'em."

Sam frowned. "Yeah. That must've been it."

"What did you do?"

"When?"

"To agitate 'em."

"I took off my clothes."

Donnie Shoes' face wrinkled up. "You…took off your *clothes*? In front of four big, dumb muscle heads? Why the hell would ya do somethin' that stupid?"

"They told me to."

"They *what*?"

"It's a long story. I really don't want to go into it right now."

Donnie Shoes nodded. "No problem. Actually, the only thing I'm concerned about is that idiot boyfriend of yours. I'll make it simple. You tell me where he is? I'll letcha go. Right here, on the spot. You'll get your clothes back and my sincere apology. I'll even give ya a few bucks for your troubles, a complimentary bottle of my finest champagne, and a limo ride back to where you live."

"And if I *don't* tell you where he is?"

Donnie Shoes sighed and shook his head. "That'd be awfully bad and stupid. See, I'm a businessman. When someone threatens one of my investments, I gotta do what's necessary to fix things. Your boyfriend threatened two of my investments and upset a bunch of the wrong people, several of 'em my best customers. I can't have somethin' like that happenin'. It's bad for business. I'm sure ya understand."

Sam's heart sank. Because of Senyllia, he was stuck here. Forever.

"Yeah. I understand."

"Good. We're on the same page, then. So now you can tell me. Where's your boyfriend?"

"You wouldn't believe me."

"Try me."

"All I can say is this. You'll never see Sam Hughes again."

"That's all you're gonna tell me?"

"That's all I *can* tell you."

With a creaking of joints, Donnie Shoes slowly stood. "Sorry we couldn't come to a mutual agreement. I guess you'll be stayin' here, then."

"Here? In this room?"

"I'll have one of my accountants bring up the necessary papers for you to sign."

"Papers?"

"Like I said, I gotta take care of my investments. Since I can't use your boyfriend to fix things, I got no choice but use you instead. Which is fine and dandy with me. See, you're one prime investment yourself."

"Thanks a lot."

"I'm sincere. I also got eyes. I use 'em all the time. In this business, you really got to. You're a sweet-lookin' bitch. I can see why my boys went apeshit when they saw ya naked. You'll be good for business. Course, ya won't be able to dance till those bruises heal up. But once they do, you'll be one of my best ladies. I'll have Nicole or Marsha give ya a few tips on how to move. Then you'll be fine. We'll start ya out in Silver, see what you can do. If you're good, and if the customers like ya, you'll be moved to Gold in no time. My best ladies are in Platinum, but they been here a while. We'll see. You're good-lookin' enough for Platinum, but we gotta wait for those bruises and welts to heal first. *Capisc?*"

"What'll I do...while they're healing?" Sam asked in an uneasy voice.

Donnie Shoes chuckled. "No problem. You'll stay right here."

Sam's heart pounded. He suspected he hadn't yet learned the worst of his horrors. "And?"

Donnie Shoes pulled open the door. "You'll entertain our customers in this room."

"Right...*here*?"

"Shouldn't be a problem." He waved an arm. "It ain't a bad room. You got a bed. There's even a tiny bathroom right over there, next to the closet. All ya need to do good in this business is a great face, pouty lips, a nice set of knockers, and a pussy." He chuckled, then moved toward the doorway. He turned around and gave Sam a wink. "Even a blind dude can see that ya got all that."

Chapter 17

After Donnie Shoes had left, Sam lay in bed, thinking of Senyllia with a renewed hatred building in his gut.

A vile, disgusting bitch. A dirty, filthy, sulfur-smelling slut. The worst kind of demon, even for Hell...

He didn't even care that she could hear his thoughts. He knew she heard them because they were connected. She said so herself. They were joined together and always would be. Sam was her servant, and she always knew everything her servants were saying and doing. Where they were, who they were with. Their connection was the invisible cord she had wrapped around his spiritual form during his first visit. It was strong and unbreakable—one that would last forever. And all she had to do to get him back was tug on it.

She could pull him back down there at any time, just as she'd done three times before. But he no longer cared because he knew she wouldn't. She had placed the ultimate hex on him and would thoroughly enjoy the fruits of his predicament.

But even though he detested her with every fiber of his being, he knew she had been right about one thing.

He was an idiot. A moron.

Only an idiot would think Hell was Heaven. Only a moron would think that just because you were able to boff any woman who crossed your path, you had achieved ultimate happiness. Only a stupid fool would think that he had come back from Hell with powers all mortal men dreamed about. And that everything was fine and right in this new, lust-filled world. And that--

A knock on the door.

Startled, he sat up.

Another knock.

"Who...is it?"

The door opened.

A round, lined face appeared in the opening. Two small, blinking dark eyes focused on him, growing instantly.

"Yes?"

"You're...Samantha?"

Sam sighed tiredly. He resisted the urge to scream. To tell whoever it was to leave him alone. But he knew better. "Yeah."

The door opened wider. A short, elderly man with thinning gray hair, thick black brows, and a large, beaky nose came in and closed the door behind him. He was dressed in a black tailor-made two-piece suit, cream-colored tie, and brown patent-leather shoes. A white carnation blossomed regally from his lapel. He looked about seventy-five. He was thickset but carried himself well. Gold rings adorned two fingers on each hand. A glittering gold watch encircled his left wrist.

He looked like an undertaker. Sam wanted to tell him that he had come to the wrong place.

The man continued staring at Sam, his eyes lowering to Sam's chest, then to his legs, which showed beneath the robe. Then, finally, the man's eyes returned to Sam's face.

"Something wrong?"

The old man shook his head slowly. "Nothing. Everything's terrific. *Perfecto. Sexy e squisito!* Dominic has indeed spoken the truth!"

Sam suddenly realized he had just been evaluated again. It was going to take time to get used to this. Me seldom experienced it. Most females are most likely accustomed to it by the time they enter grade school.

"Is that all you came for?"

He blinked himself out of his trance. His lined cheeks flushed. "I am Giorgio DeAngelis. I happen to own this establishment."

Sam shrugged. "You've got a nice place here." He didn't know what else to say.

"Thank you." DeAngelis continued to stare.

"Why are you here?" Sam asked uneasily. "To tell me you're my boss?"

"Partly. I've also come to look over my manager's latest investment." He nodded approvingly. "I am happy to see that he has not exaggerated."

"Thanks. It makes my day. You can go now."

"Not so fast. May I call you Samantha?"

"Sure. Knock yourself out. What do I call you? Mr. D? Giorgio? Boss?"

"Boss will be fine."

"Good. Nice seeing you. Boss."

"I've also come for another reason."

Sam swallowed. He was afraid to ask. "Which is?"

DeAngelis chuckled as he unbuttoned his jacket. "To sample the merchandise, of course!"

Sam couldn't reply.

DeAngelis stood, took off his jacket, and folded it very neatly over the back of the armchair. "Dominic has said you are one special, valuable asset." Then he sat and unbuckled his belt. "Once again I must see if he has spoken the truth."

***

"Dominic has spoken the truth. You are indeed one very special, valuable asset."

Giorgio DeAngelis sat in the chair, fastening his belt. A stupid grin covered his face.

Massaging his aching jaw, Sam got up and went to sit on the bed. He turned away while he wiped his wet cheeks and chin. He also felt some wetness on his left earlobe and wiped it as well. He felt filthy and humiliated and didn't want to look at the old man right now. That old boy's silly grin made Sam want to deck the bastard.

"Yes. You're really very, very good, lady. *Fantastico*. The best! Dominic did not exaggerate." The old man got up, carefully picked up his jacket, unfolded it, and slipped it back on.

"You're welcome." Sam wanted to add "asshole" to the end of his statement. He decided against it. Insulting the boss of this operation would be disastrous. So would decking him. They couldn't kill him, but they sure could bust him up even worse than they already had. He didn't want to spend eternity with his jaw wired shut.

DeAngelis meticulously adjusted his jacket and sat back down. "Know what I really enjoyed?"

"Don't care."

"I really like how you use your tongue--"

"That's all right."

"But I feel the need to tell you--"

"Why?"

The old man grinned devilishly. Sam had a feeling he wasn't going to like the man's reply.

"So you know to do it the very same way the next time."

The next time…

Damn, damn, damn!

Sam's temples pounded. His blood boiled. He felt his hands squeezing into fists. Maybe he could just quietly strangle the bastard before sneaking out through the window. It might not be that difficult. The old man would probably do anything Sam asked him to. Getting him to hand over his expensive tie might be a cakewalk. Or his belt. And the window looked like it was functional. It would probably ease open without making *too* much racket.

"The next time, I'd like it to be in a different--"

"I don't want to *hear* it, okay?" Getting on your knees and servicing a fat, rich idiot for money had to be the ultimate humiliation. Especially when you were a guy and the rich idiot thought you were really a babe.

The experience had been bad enough. A graphic recap wouldn't exactly help the situation.

"As you wish..."

"Just leave, okay?"

DeAngelis didn't budge.

"Did you hear me?"

The old man frowned. "I own this club, you know..."

"Yeah. I vaguely recall you mentioning that." Sam rubbed his eyes. It was bad enough that he had to handle this jerk's undersized dick. Now he had to listen to his accomplishments. How the hell did women endure this shit without throwing up or blowing their brains out?

"I'm very well off."

Sam wanted this old fart out of here. He didn't want to hear his success story. He wanted to brush his teeth. And gargle with a sharp mouthwash. And he badly needed a shower. He also wanted a good, strong drink. "Good for you."

"I'm a multi-millionaire."

"Terrific. I'm extremely happy for you. Now go. Bye-bye."

"I can afford to give you whatever you wish."

This old coot was really grating on Sam's nerves. "*Now* you tell me. And here I was, holding back."

DeAngelis fished through his trouser pocket, pulled out his wallet, and opened it. He took out a few bills, put the wallet back, then approached the bed. "Here's five hundred."

Sam stared at the wad of bills trapped between the man's arthritic fingers. "That's a lot of money for a...for what I just did."

DeAngelis handed it to him. "There's plenty more where that came from."

Sam didn't want to touch the old bastard's money. Judging by the hex Senyllia had put on him, he suspected something foul would happen.

"Go ahead. Take it."

"Why?"

"I want you to have it."

"What else do I have to do?"

DeAngelis shrugged. "Nothing."

"Nothing?"

A wink. "Not right now..."

Okay. Here it comes. Best get this out in the open before I can make another huge blunder. "What's your angle?"

"My angle?"

"The money. Your telling me I don't have to do anything else. For right now. What's going on?"

"You like it here?"

"What are you? Crazy?"

DeAngelis just smiled.

"Of course not. I absolutely *don't* like it here. I *hate* it here."

"How would you like your own place?"

Sam blinked. "My...own *place*?"

"I'd like to buy you an apartment."

"An apartment?"

The old man shrugged. "You know. A place of your own, where you'd live by yourself."

194

"You're kidding..."

A nod. "I'd like you to be--"

"Your whore?"

DeAngelis sighed. "That's a crude way of putting it, I guess..."

Sam continued staring. The old man looked sincere, yet this reeked.

"How old are you?" Sam asked.

DeAngelis stiffened. "What's that have to do with--"

"Just answer the question."

"Sixty-sev--"

"The truth, dammit."

DeAngelis scowled. "You sure are one gutsy lady. Seventy-five."

"Don't you think you're a tad old for me?"

The scowl remained. "You realize if you were a guy talking to me like that, I'd have your balls?"

Sam knew better than reply. He just shrugged.

"You want outa here or not?"

"What if I do?"

"So...do we have a deal?" He held out his hand.

Sam stared at the old man's hand. What the hell... It might just get him the hell out of here. He reluctantly shook it.

DeAngelis grinned. "You got helluva grip for a female."

"It comes from holding onto things so you don't get ripped off."

DeAngelis nodded. "I like a good grip on a babe."

Sam stared at the man. He couldn't believe any of this. He was now a mob boss's girlfriend. His kept woman. His whore. The "lady no one else will mess with."

But he had to ask. "Why me?"

DeAngelis shrugged. "I've already told you. You're one hot lady."

"That's it?"

"You're sassy. And tough. And you know how to fire up an old man, then put it out just as he likes it. You know exactly what a guy wants. How to handle him." DeAngelis stopped talking and stared at him suspiciously. "Sure you weren't a guy in a past life?"

Sam didn't reply.

"Anyway, that should answer your question, right?"

"Yeah. It answers my question."

"Then take this money. I gotta make a quick call to Donnie Shoes and tell him to bring your clothes up so I can take you outa here." He pulled his hand back. "You do want outa here, right?"

"Yeah. I do want outa here."

The old man held out the bills. "Wouldn't wanna take a babe somewhere she don't wanna go."

Sam gave the room a quick glance. And the unmade bed. And the cheap furniture. And the ill-fitting bathrobe they'd left for him.

As if his hand belonged to someone else, he eagerly reached out and snatched the bills.

EPILOGUE

Giorgio DeAngelis owned nearly a dozen condominiums and apartment complexes in the Central Florida area. One of them, a twenty-four-unit complex of luxury Winter Park condominiums, boasted all the modern conveniences, including an Olympic-sized pool, an impressive recreation hall, two tennis courts, and a shuffleboard court. It sat within walking distance of two shopping malls, several of the town's finest restaurants, and an exclusive health spa that catered to women.

Sam's new condo, a spacious two-bedroom unit, backed up to the pool. The unit was comfortable, well-furnished, and secluded. It was twice the size of Sam's old place and much ritzier than Sam could have ever afforded on his own.

Sam appreciated Giorgio's generosity but realized such a wonderful gift would not come without obligation. And now, recognized by everyone as a beautiful, sexy young woman, he knew full well what that obligation would be.

"What kind of car would you like?" Giorgio asked the day Sam moved in.

Certain he hadn't heard the old man's question correctly, Sam said, "What did you say?"

"I just asked you what kind of car--"

"My last ride was a Camaro--"

"I didn't ask you *that*. I asked, what kind of car would you like to have?"

197

Sam shrugged. "I've always liked the looks of the new Challenger."

"What color?"

"Color?" Once again he didn't think his hearing was working quite right.

"Red? Blue? Black? Silver?"

Sam shrugged. "I've always been fond of emerald green."

Early the next morning, a brand-new, tricked out emerald green Challenger sat in the paved drive, a large red ribbon fastened to its long, sloped hood.

Sam couldn't believe his luck. He took the keys from DeAngelis, drove up and down Semoran Boulevard, then to the local mall, where he spent a thousand bucks on jeans, tee shirts, underwear, and three pairs of shoes. And as a token of gratitude for Giorgio's kindness, a see-through nightie, high-heeled pumps, and some really sexy ladies' underwear.

Since they hurt his feet, Sam wore the pumps only on rare occasions. He slipped on the underwear when Giorgio called to say he was coming for his evening visit. It wasn't much of a sacrifice. When the old man stopped by in his silver Rolls, he usually came on a Friday night, slept late, then went back to his office the next morning after breakfast to conduct his business affairs.

The evening's entertainment was simple and not very stressful—at least, not for Sam. Sam put Giorgio's favorite piece of music, Ravel's *Bolero*, on the stereo and then indulged in a few minutes of the same suggestive moves he had seen Wendy and

198

Nicole perform in the Platinum Room. Giorgio eagerly watched from the La-Z-Boy, then accompanied Sam to the bedroom.

Sam quickly discovered that if he did the moves well enough, Giorgio popped quickly, then fell instantly to sleep. And since the old man was well over seventy, he never woke during the night for an encore performance.

Sam spent his days watching his favorite programs on the 60-inch widescreen and sitting by the complex pool, acquiring a terrific tan. The old man wanted him darkly tanned, and since Sam had always enjoyed relaxing in the Florida sun, he saw no reason to argue.

Since Sam spent so much time at the complex, he was able to make friends with several young women living there. Two of his new friends also spent a great deal of time at the pool. Anna, the brunette, worked at her home computer business, while her partner Stacy drove to Orlando each day to run her fashion business. Since the girls were party animals and thoroughly enjoyed threesomes, Sam was in his glory. He and the girls frequently engaged in three-way sex, bondage, humiliation, water sports, suspension, femdom, erotic asphyxiation, and rubber ware.

Despite Senyllia's hex, another dream had been fulfilled.

Sam was always back at the condo when Giorgio stopped by for his visits. He had learned that after three glasses of good wine and fifteen minutes of watching Sam move to the sexy strains of *Bolero*, Giorgio almost always nodded off and slept the night away in the La-Z-Boy.

Sam learned early on that he thoroughly enjoyed this new lavish, undemanding life. He could run around town, doing whatever he wanted, and had more than enough money to suit his needs. Giorgio had given him his own checking account with a running balance of ten thousand bucks. And since the old man was easy to satisfy, Sam had no problem fulfilling Giorgio's desires. When Sam felt some pressure building up from Senyllia, he wandered over to Anna's for an afternoon quickie, or an all-night threesome with Anna and Stacy. Or Melissa's place at the other end of the complex, to fulfill her needs while her husband was deployed overseas. Or Connie, the stunning fortyish blonde who lived by herself across the street, trying to repair her life since her rich husband had dumped her for a younger woman.

Giorgio went on business trips at least twice a month. When he had first asked Sam to accompany him on a two-day jaunt to Miami Beach, Sam eagerly agreed. It gave him the chance to hook up with even more hot bisexual ladies while the old man was busy conducting his business. But when Sam was approached at the bar by a slew of well-dressed men and given free drinks, then handed hotel room keys, Giorgio decided it would be much safer to keep his special lady back at their penthouse apartment, where she'd be safe and out of harm's way.

Giorgio let Sam do whatever he wished. He didn't mind when Sam said he liked to go shopping so he could be by himself. Giorgio also didn't mind that Sam enjoyed watching kick-ass movies…and didn't like to be cooped up in the apartment very long…and was able to get the old man off in just a few minutes.

Giorgio went along with everything. In the old man's view, Sam was one hot lady. She was better than anything Donnie Shoes had in the club. Giorgio liked having his woman in her own place, where he could see her whenever he wished and take her out to dinner whenever the mood struck him.

It was the perfect setup. Giorgio and his wife of fifty years lived in his lakeside estate in Winter Springs. After having four kids and suffering through three miscarriages, Della no longer wanted sex or even cared about satisfying her husband's urges. If he had other interests, so be it. As long as she had the house and total access to her own checking account, she was happy as a clam.

And as long as Giorgio had his own young beauty living in one of his condos, he too was happy.

And so was Sam. He finally realized that he *had* found his own personal version of Heaven.

He also understood what it truly meant to be a woman.

And judging by the fact that he had never again been sent back down to Hell, he knew that he had finally achieved Senyllia's complete approval.